Best
Vegan
Science Fiction
& Fantasy

2017

Also from Metaphorosis Books

Best Vegan Science Fiction & Fantasy

2017

edited by
B. Morris Allen

ISBN: 978-1-64076-001-1 (e-book)
ISBN: 978-1-64076-002-8 (paperback)

plant
based
press

from
Metaphorosis Publishing

Neskowin

Contents

From the Editor

I'm writing this in Belgrade, Serbia, hardly a bastion of progressive animal rights philosophy. Yet even here, cute pro-vegan pictures of pigs, chickens, cows, and foxes are strewn across the city. In the few years since I lived here full time, vegan and vegan-friendly restaurants have exploded – from essentially one to half a dozen or more. It's always been possible to eat *posno* (Lenten – largely vegan) in Belgrade. But now it's not just a religious label but a recognized life choice.

That's not to say there's not a backlash. Inevitably, as with any suddenly popular issue, there is. Already, restaurants are shifting from 'vegan' to 'plant-based'. The food is the same, but the philosophy is different.

As someone who's been vegan for quite a long time, I've watched the changes with some bemusement. Overall, though, it's a good thing. At the very least, more people have an idea what veganism is about, even if they dismiss it as a silly fad.

All that is to say that, despite its ups and downs, the world is, in many ways, getting better. It's a meandering process, but there's still a chance we'll survive ourselves, and some other species may too.

The stories in this anthology give cause for optimism. They're not all happy stories; some are frightening, some grim, some melancholy. But they're all vegan – in the sense that they don't include use of animals for human benefit. They weren't mostly written by vegans, or even intended to be vegan. But they are. Reading them, you'll spend some time in vegan worlds –

worlds where we've resolved at least one major problem. Relax in those worlds; enjoy them. Then come out fortified to face the real world and make better futures possible.

B. Morris Allen
Editor

Bluebird

Benjamin Cort

Nelson Towers spent most of his time oiling the feathers. When he had taken the job he had been enticed by the prestige, the travel, and the pay. He quickly came to realize that his work was to be reviled, not celebrated, that everyplace he traveled was more depressing than the last, and that he was mostly paid to oil the feathers. But at least the pay was good.

In the early days he had worked with a small penlight, its thin beam shaking nervously in a sweaty palm. He tried to use it sparingly, but the shape of the wings was foreign to him, and he often found himself flicking it on and marveling at their rough form. He worked when it slept, which was often. He dreaded being in its presence.

Now he worked in total darkness. He knew how it lay as it slept and where to step as he moved around it. It hungrily lapped up oil and soaked it deep into its plumage. For a thing that spent most of its time sleeping in dark, quiet places, it needed to be constantly fed.

He hadn't looked at it in weeks. He had never seen the whole thing at once, nor did he want to. When he worked, it slept. When it worked, he turned away.

Saying that Lexington had let itself go would have been an overstatement. Towers had always considered the town to be a dump. It now just had the outward appearance to reflect that.

He had tracked it here from Harper's Ferry over the course of two long days, and each mile North turned his mood darker. The sky too, darkened with his countenance. Fall this far North was never pleasant, and the road was full of packed cars trundling South. Sleepy children ogled his truck as it drove carelessly over the dotted white lines. His whole side of the highway was barren. It seemed as if the entire North had packed its bags and moved out. Towers was used to this by now. He tried not to take it personally.

When he finally pulled into Lexington Center, it was night. His digital watch read 11:04 in garish green numbers. The buildings hung low with muted colors. The store windows were dark. Some had been smashed in, revealing emptied shelves. This strip was dominated by banks, boutiques, and frozen yogurt stores. Towers slowed his truck down at the intersection. It would be around here somewhere. He switched off the engine and hopped out, leaving the truck in the middle of the road.

In the back, wedged between large drums of oil, his little printer whirred and spat out a sheet of paper. He tore it from the machine. "St. Cuthbert," it read, simply. The smartest, richest, and most powerful people in the entire world had gathered in the City and built an array of satellites that could track both its and his position every second of every day to the meter. He had been given a printer with a radio duct-taped to the side. The City loved to cut costs for people who didn't matter. Towers crumpled up the paper and tossed it into the street.

Leaves crunched under his feet as he plodded over to the sidewalk. Three days ago the square would have been bustling. The restaurants would have rolled out their patios to soak in the last few days of warmth left in the season and the air would have filled been with warm light, idle chatter, and wisps of cigarette smoke. There would be a line out the movie theater door for the eight o'clock showing of whatever was on. Kids would be lounging around the large green lawn in front of the church, waiting for some interesting trouble to spring to their minds.

The church's facade had always made him nervous. But Allison had loved the lawn, so he had pretended to love it too. When they were younger, they would chase each other around it in endless loops. When they were older, they would sit against the trunks of the trees, talking for hours in the shade.

The lawn was filled with leaves now. Towers walked across it, his hands jammed deep into the pockets of his brown jacket. The stained glass face of Mr. Christ stared down at him. Towers lingered outside and met his eyes defiantly. Now it was Towers who had the upper hand. When the bird was done with this town there would be nothing left. He turned off his glowing watch and tried the door. It opened inward to his touch, and he slipped inside quickly, closing it behind him.

The Church of Saint Cuthbert was dark. He could see high above him hints of starry sky through the colored glass. And he could hear it breathing. He hadn't been able to detect its soft, fluttering breaths, at first. He hadn't even thought that it needed to breathe. Now, like it or not, the sound of its breath was the sound of his home.

Towers approached it, ducking under a sharp wing. He moved slowly, feeling his way through the darkness. It had moved the pews aside to fit its bulk into the space just below the pulpit. He sat gingerly on the edge of one of the pews and reached out a soft hand. He stroked the side of its face, feeling its feathers prick him as he did. It was thirsty. He stuck his index finger into his mouth and sucked the blood away. He walked back to his truck, pulled an oil barrel onto his little cart, and wheeled it back to the church. He worked till just before sunrise, then returned to his truck. He smoked a cigarette and threw the butt into the street. It smoldered on the asphalt, the square's single spot of light. He watched it burn out slowly.

Towers slept deeply, and woke at eight as his watch alarm beeped. It was dark. He had a cot in the back of his truck, but he often slept in the front seat, as he had last night. It was probably the hunger that had woken him, or perhaps just the loud rumbling of his stomach. There was a peanut butter and jelly sandwich in his glove compartment, but when he opened it it was all squashed and malformed. He slammed the compartment shut. There was always other food somewhere.

He rolled out onto the street and immediately felt his legs go wobbly. He leaned against the side of his truck and gave himself a moment to fully reenter to world of the waking. His neck was killing him, and he rolled it back and forth a few times. When he was young, he had been told never to do a full rotation, or he'd hurt himself. How or why that would happen had never been explained, but he was still careful.

When his legs were behaving again, he made his creaking way down the strip, past the church, and into the wooded streets of Lexington. He hadn't set out with a specific goal in mind, just that of getting some food from somewhere, but he quickly realized where his legs had begun to take him. He had had a lot of firsts in this town. Why not say one last goodbye to the house of his first love? Besides, they had always fed him well. They might have left something good behind.

He took a break at the top of Weeks Street, perched at the peak of the small hill there. These streets felt the same as they always did. Quiet. He flicked his penlight on. Even back when he lived here, he had needed light to navigate. The streetlights were few and far in between, the streets badly paved and lined with ditches and trees, and when the sun set it did so completely.

He used to sneak out late at night, and scurry across this exact route. There was a tree in Allison's yard he could scurry up to reach her bedroom. Or sometimes she'd meet him in the woods, and they'd spend the night wandering. Of course his starting point had been different, back then, but that house had been knocked down and paved over a long time ago. Time had changed the shape of the route. Trees had fallen and slopes eroded. Feet stamped down new paths. He cut from street to yard to forest and back to street, his feet unsteadily but automatically moving dutifully below him.

He was so carefully looking down that it took him until he stepped from the sidewalk to the short trimmed green grass of the front lawn to notice what was wrong. He could see the grass. How green it was. He looked up in bewilderment. The front windows of the house were awash with light, a latticed shadow scattered across the yard. There was never light. Why would there be light? The electric companies should have turned off the power a long time ago. Mr. Song had always had a backup generator; he was always very proud when the power went out but the house stayed lit. But it couldn't have run for this long without being refueled.

"Who is it!" A voice called out, more accusation than question.

Towers's head pounded. He hadn't heard another voice in so long. He opened his mouth to respond but found his mouth dry and his tongue fuzzy. He coughed, unable to form coherent vocals. He hadn't spoken in longer.

"I warn you, I'm armed," the voice threatened.

Towers stood rooted in place. His cough was really working its way through him now, heaving out big wracking lungfuls of air. He put a hand up in a placating manner, vaguely in the direction of the house's second story.

"I'm coming out!" The voice warned, and Towers heard the front door slamming open. He looked up, but the bright windows were ruining his night vision and all he could make out was a large black shape barreling towards him. The shape skidded to a halt a few yards away, brandishing an implement in a threatening manner. "Jesus, is that you, Nel?"

Towers seemed to have regained some control of his breath and managed to squeeze out a raspy "yes," before beginning to convulse in coughs again. The shape, now clearly a broad shouldered man was a carefully combed over patch of white hair, approached and laid a hand on his shoulder. Towers flinched away, but felt a firm grip of fingers squeeze tight.

"You don't look so good, Nel," the man muttered. "Get inside, I'll get you a drink."

Towers felt himself ushered through the door and into the gleaming house. The front door led directly into the dining room. He had always felt uncomfortable at meals because of this. The looming door implied to him that they were always expecting company. Mr. Song pushed him around the table and into the kitchen beyond, which spilled out into the living room. A staircase wound its way up to the second floor or their left. The back door stood, locked, on their right. Mr. Song laid the rifle on the kitchen table. He opened a cabinet and threw Towers a bottle of water. "There, that should help."

Towers hastily tore the cap off and gulped the water down gratefully. Drinking was such a vital process that he surprised himself with how long he could forget to do it. He crinkled the empty plastic sheepishly, raising it in a half salute. "Thank you," the sound of his own voice was strange, but he liked it. "I guess I needed that."

Mr. Song was looking him up and down with a blank face that Towers couldn't quite read. The man had always made him nervous. He had never felt as if he had earned his trust. "Little Nel," Mr. Song murmured. "Haven't heard from you since you ran off to college."

"It was hard to keep in touch," Towers shrugged. It hadn't been. He didn't know what had stopped him. He suspected that he was a coward. He did know that he hated being called Nel. He hated Nelson more. He had always liked Towers though. Short, strong. Towers and Song. They had fit well together.

A woman appeared in the stairway. Her long red hair had gone straight with age and was held back in a loose bun. She looked tired. And very angry. Mr. Song turned to her. "Look who showed up!" he said, loudly.

Mrs. Song looked into Towers's eyes, and he immediately felt too uncomfortable to meet her gaze. "Nel," she breathed out. "I didn't think we'd ever see you again."

"Neither did I," Towers replied, his heart beginning to pound. "Why are you still here?"

Mr. Song frowned. "Because it's my house." Mrs. Song glowered at him. "Sorry," he corrected himself. "Our house. It's our house! I'm not letting the City take that from us just because that idiot President said they could." He took a few deep breaths. Towers put the empty water bottle down. He very much wished that he had not come here. "But what are you doing here, Nel? Are you looking for Allison?"

Towers shook his head. "No."

"Well, good, she's long gone. Virginia. College too. You would've known that if you had called her, Nel." Towers smiled awkwardly. He glanced at Mrs. Song. Her visage was stone. Mr. Song frowned. "So why are you here?"

Towers paused. No use lying. "I followed the bird," he said. His voice came out low and raspy, almost a whisper.

Mrs. Song didn't move. "Followed the—" Mr. Song repeated, lost. Then his face hardened. "So that's what they taught you at that school. How to sell out your home to the City."

"Actually," Towers found himself correcting, "I work for Drummel. Which is owned by the Hollis Corporation, which is owned by Nanover, which is owned by the Echo Conglomerate. No one works for 'the City.'"

"We're not leaving," Mr. Song stated bluntly. His fingers twitched. Towers took a step back towards the door, pretending to adjust his stance.

"You have to, Mr. Song," Towers said. "All of you." He glanced at Mrs. Song, who had turned her gaze to her husband. "It's pointless. Everyone knows that. Tomorrow morning there won't be anything left."

"We are leaving," Mrs. Song put bluntly. Towers's head jerked towards her. She stood stock still, and her gaze was so caustic he was briefly worried that he might turn to stone himself.

Mr. Song turned away from them, and hunched his shoulders over the kitchen table. His fingers found the rifle's stock. "I will not leave," he said vehemently. Towers couldn't tell if he was addressing Towers, his wife, or himself. "I worked for forty years to buy this house from the bank. It's mine. No one can take it. Not even the City."

"Then don't come," Mrs. Song shrugged. Towers suspected that this was not the first time they had had this discussion. She turned to Towers. "I hear people like us are going West. That there's still something on the coast. Do you know if that's true?"

Towers nodded. "I know some people are going there. So there's something. For now. I don't know what."

"Something is better than nothing. It was nice to see you again, Nel. I'll be upstairs, packing." She climbed the stairs and was gone.

Mr. Song waited until she left, and then picked up the rifle. He turned quickly and aimed it at Towers. His face was impassive. Towers shot his hands up. "Come on, Mr. Song," he pleaded.

"What if I just shoot you right now?" Mr. Song asked.

"They would send someone else. It would take another week, but it would all be gone just the same. And they'd send you to prison for life when they found out what you did."

"Who would send someone?"

"Drummel," Towers replied.

Mr. Song took a step towards Towers. "What if I shoot you now, and then shoot whoever is in charge over at Drummel." Towers moved to speak again, but Mr. Song cut him off. "Maybe not me. But maybe another angry man does. What then?"

"Hollis would promote someone new, and they would send someone else, and Lexington is gone all the same," Towers said.

Mr. Song lowered the rifle. He looked tired. Towers felt a surge of pity for the man. "Why are you doing this, Nel? This is your home too."

Towers shrugged. "It's a job, and someone's going to fill the position. What does it matter if it's me? I might as well be the one getting paid."

"How much, Nel?"

"Enough to live on. You need to get out of here, Mr. Song. It isn't safe."

Mr. Song let the rifle drop back onto the kitchen table. "What's the point, Nel? There's nothing for me in the City. I'm too old. And you'll just catch up to me, eventually."

"You can go West, Mr. Song," Towers felt himself pleading with the man. "There're something for people like us," he cut himself off, and frowned. "Like you out there. There's still work."

Mr. Song was shaking his head. "No, no there isn't. Not for me. I worked in the same library for forty years, Nel. Just down the street. What would I do out there?"

Towers shrugged. "Live." Mr. Song lowered himself heavily into one of the kitchen chairs. Towers took the chair across from him. "I didn't pick this place. I wouldn't have picked this place. But the City did. People like us, Mr. Song? We don't get to make choices anymore. People like me follow the bird. People like you run from her shadow. You're right, there's nothing for you out there like the life you used to have. And if the City had anything for you, you wouldn't be here now. But that's no reason to stay. Go be with your family."

"What do you care what happens to me?" Mr. Song wasn't looking at him, really. He seemed to be focused on the old electric clock on the other end of the kitchen. Towers didn't have to turn to see it. Its black hands floated above a brightly lit blue face.

"I spent more time here than I did in my own home," Towers said. Mr. Song frowned. "You didn't ask for a third child, but you let me know I was always welcome." Towers rose. "Goodbye Mr. Song." On the way out he noticed that the dining room table had been set for four. He shuddered, and left through the front door.

On his way back Towers climbed through the broken window of a gas station and helped himself to some stale power bars from a display in the back. He crossed the street to the old high school. A looming, brick building, it had never laid claim to anything special, neither architecturally nor academically. Towers went around to the side and sat on a wooden bench that overlooked the soccer field. Taking advantage of a rare gap in the tree cover, the moon shone down on the grass. He unwrapped a power bar and bit into it.

"Sit down with me," Towers called out into the night.

A boy joined him on the bench. He hungrily took in Towers's features, from the rough main of stubble to the blackness under his nails to the rings under his eyes.

"Why didn't you come downstairs?" Towers asked.

The boy chewed on his lip. "Mom wouldn't let me." Towers offered him a power bar. The boy waved it down. "I don't want to leave, Nel." Towers flashed him a look. "Sorry, Towers." He rolled his eyes. "She got to call you Nel."

Towers threw away the first wrapper and cracked a second. "Doesn't matter what you want, Sam. I want an office job, with fresh coffee every morning, but I took a test and it told me I wasn't smart enough, so here I am instead."

Sam bore down on his lip in silence. Towers finished his second bar. "How is she?" he asked at last.

"I think she's fine. She's at college. Virginia."

"I came here from Virginia."

"Oh?" Sam asked. Then his face hardened. "Oh." He kicked at the dirt. "Is there anything left?"

"No. Nothing. It's all the City's now. But most people got out." They lapsed into uncomfortable silence for a few minutes before Towers could find any more words. "Did she ever talk about me?" Towers put down the rest of the bars. He had lost his appetite.

"We didn't talk much," Sam said. Towers narrowed his eyes. The goalpost was catching the moonlight and shining a brilliant white in the darkness. "You never called."

"I know."

"Come with us, Nel. We can find her."

Towers shook his head. "I'm not your brother, Sam."

"But," Sam started to say, before Towers cut him off.

"No. I have a job to do."

"What happens when you've been everywhere?"

"Haven't been everywhere yet." Towers moved to his feet. Sam scampered up after him. Towers's eyes had fallen onto the dark shape of the high school. "I'm sorry you never got the chance to go. It was good there. I think I may have peaked there. If happiness is any metric. I don't think it is anymore."

"Can I see it?"

"See what?"

"You know."

Towers started walking. "Sure."

"No lights. Just listen." The church rose up in front of them. He and Samuel Song had been here together many times before. The circumstances weren't too different. Just worship of a different power.

"Can't I just see it for one second? Please?" Sam asked.

"No." Towers said. "No lights on her, not even for a moment."

Sam relented and nodded. Then, his eyebrows knitted together. "Her?"

Towers paused, hand on the wide doors. He shrugged. "I call her Bluebird." Can a machine be alive? He wasn't sure, but he had been alone with her for so long.

"Why?"

"My mother told me that bluebirds steal eggs from other birds. I thought that was very sad when I was little. Still," he pushed the doors open, and lowered his voice to a whisper. "They are beautiful, aren't they? Take my hand."

Towers led Sam into the dark church. The Bluebird shifted as she slept. She was hungry, and she was almost ready. Towers liked to imagine that she could dream. Perhaps she dreamed of a tired man with soft hands. He took Sam to a pew in the back and sat him down. "Don't move, don't make a sound," he whispered.

Her wings had unfurled since the last time he was here. He stepped inside of them and felt their faint heat around him. He ran his hand along their length. His palm bled. She sighed in her sleep. She must be hungry. She always needed so much oil before she worked. Sam fidgeted in the back. Towers sat inside of its wings and leaned against her, waiting out the minutes in silence.

This was wrong. Silently, he moved back to where Sam was sitting, took his hand, and led him from the church. Outside, Sam frowned at the blood and wiped his hand on the door, leaving a red print behind.

Towers folded his arms. "You need to leave."

Sam nodded. But he lingered. "Is it true though, what they say about them?"

"That what?"

"That it was an accident. Discovering them."

Towers smiled. "I used to think that too."

"Used to?"

"Yeah. Used to." He put a finger on the streak of blood on the door, tracing its path down the grain. "I think I wanted to believe that we wouldn't willfully make something so..." he stopped, and took his hand back, wiping it clean on the back of his pants. "Well, anyway, we would. We did. It's a new world, the City. It's better there. But it doesn't care about the old world out here. And it won't stop growing until there's nothing of the old world left." He looked Sam in the eye. The younger boy turned away. "You have to go, Sam."

Sam nodded, mostly to himself. "This is it, then?"

"Yeah."

"I don't know what to say, Nel."

"Me neither."

"Goodbye, I guess." Sam stuck out a hand, and Towers awkwardly took it. Blood squeezed out from between their fingers.

"If you see her," Towers began. But then he stopped. He had no idea where that thought had been headed.

"What?"

"Nothing. Don't tell her about me."

Sam looked away uncomfortably. Then he reached into his pocket and took out a watch. It was battered and cheap, and light in Towers's palm as Sam handed it to him. "I found it in her room," Sam said, still not meeting the older boy's eyes. "It's yours, isn't it?"

Towers turned away. His eyes were wet, and his cheeks flushed with shame. "Yeah," he muttered. "Thanks."

Sam bounced from one foot to another for a few moments, and then turned to leave. The trees swallowed up his slight frame.

Towers waited outside for a few minutes, and then went back into the church. In the dark he sat, turning the watch over and over in his hand. The morning he left, he had told her how he felt. Then they kissed. Then he got in the car and drove away. "Eight o'clock tonight," he said, before he rolled the window up. "I'll call you." He took off his old watch and gave it to her. "So you know when it's eight," he said with a smile. She swapped it with her own, which was digital and sparkling new. She set an alarm on it for eight, and then gave it to him. "So you don't forget," she smiled back.

For seven years he had kept hers. He had always assumed she had done the same.

He sat there till just before the sun rose. Then he slipped out of the church, oil untouched, and went back to his truck.

Towers lit a cigarette, slid it between his lips, and started the car. He paused, his hands on the wheel, the truck idling loudly underneath him. He drove up Weeks Street and took the long way around to the house. The sun began to peek its head up from the horizon, and thin rays of light filtered through the trees as he stepped out onto the lawn. The house was dark, but he thought he saw a shadow move in one of the second story windows. It looked out across the street at the boy and his truck and then slipped away.

Towers felt a wave of bile rise up in his stomach. What pointless, destructive protest.

He drove a few miles South as the sun rose. He parked his truck on the empty highway and sat on the hood, facing North and leaning back against the windshield.

She woke. Her rising body, propelled by powerful wings, shattered the roof of the church. The steeple fell, its ringing bell cutting through the soft bird calls of the early morning. The church collapsed. The square collapsed. The trees melted. She beat her wings painfully, heavily, each pulse of devastation draining what little oil remained. She was hungry. So hungry. Towers watched. She screamed in frustration. And then she gave up, and flew North.

Towers finished his cigarette and flicked it to the ground. He felt his eyes closing, and let it happen.

He woke at noon, the sun glaring directly down into his red eyes. He licked his dry lips, pressed a hand onto his rumbling stomach, and got back into the truck. It roared to life under his touch. He would have time to take care of himself later.

When he had first taken the job he would always return when it had finished to marvel at its work. He would drive around the perfect, empty circle. No ruins, no signs of life. A clean slate. Weeks later, when he had a rare moment of free time, he would come back to see what had become of the land. Sometimes the City itself would have taken it, its shining glass buildings popping up overnight like weeds. Sometimes it would be a sleekly automated farm, or a rumbling mine, sucking the earth dry to feed the endlessly growing City.

He didn't know what Lexington would look like now. He didn't know if Weeks Street had been far enough from the church. He was too tired to care.

He took the first exit West that he could find. At the bottom of the ramp he found himself blocked by another car. He slowed, and got out of the truck.

Sam Song smiled from his perch on the hood. He turned to his mother. "See? I told you he'd come."

Mrs. Song arched an eyebrow from the front seat. Towers went around to the back of his truck and pulled the fax machine into the street. There was a printed paper in the tray, but he left it there without looking. He smashed his boot into the machine and felt it crumple under his weight. If the City needed to talk to him they could drive West themselves. Then he grabbed his cigarettes and lighter from the dashboard, stuffed them into his pockets, and left the door open and the keys in the ignition. He slid into the passenger seat of the Song's car. Mrs. Song nodded at him. He nodded back. She started the car and they slipped away.

That night, on the road, Towers was woken by his watch alarm. He looked at the bright numbers. Eight o'clock.

"Bluebird" originally appeared in *Metaphorosis*
on Friday, 27 October 2017

About the author

Benjamin Cort hopes to be a doctor sometime before he dies and drinks an unhealthy amount of tea. He spends most of his money on board games and maple cream cookies from CVS. He likes to play guitar, but doesn't do it all that well, and the majority of his musical repertoire consists of Matchbox 20 covers. He often wears a blue knit hat, given to him by a nice old lady on the Appalachian Trail, which he secretly hopes is lucky.

Ligeia is Waiting

Russell Hemmell

Life used to be like that. A wake-up call, a coffee too hot, complaints and a day at work. Add and subtract steps during weekends – anything can be written off except complaining. And celebrations, holidays, marriages and funerals, binge drinking, sport competitions and career choices.

Yes, life used to be all those things. Once upon a time, on that blue planet called Earth.

It was also the mythological era when people talked about exploring the Solar System, expanding mankind's reach beyond its original cocoon. Discovering new worlds, building unlikely colonies, testing the limit of human adaptation in hostile environments. And further.

No longer. Never again. Those days are gone.

Suit up, gear check. Impossible to go out there without running the essential telemetry routines first. No matter how long we have been doing it, the margin for errors remains zero. Not .05, .01 or even .001. It's null. A mistake, and death is mathematically assured. One of the perks of living in space. Not that many others exist.

Saturn is low on the horizon, but Enceladus is fully visible from our location on high dunes. Today is going to be nice.

"What are we waiting for?"

"For the optimal conditions. Don't behave as if you've never done it before."

More than two centuries have passed since the historical Cassini mission showed us the face of Titan, and we still find it beautiful. In spite of everything. I guess this is what it means being human. You keep marvelling. I look at the familiar view in front of my eyes, imagining how Earthians might have felt when seeing pictures of this place for the first time. Dazed, I believe. Hypnotised. Elated. Willing to go and conquer it, unaware what that dream would have translated into.With hindsight, I don't know what they actually expected. But not what they got, granted. Otherwise nobody would be here now. For reality in space is different from any prediction, no matter how grim, and that's something the last two hundred years have not changed. It's to be unable to go outdoor without a spacesuit, a sophisticate life support, and triple checking for any bug, biological or software-based. It's never being alone out there, into the wild, because the risk of malfunctioning is simply too much for a single person to handle. It means a dull life, slaving in sterilised, comfortable but anodyne environments, where nothing's worth a day on Earth, swimming into the blue ocean and breathing without a mask.

"That's not my usual scene."

"No, but you're here, as strange as it might look to me. So you'd better do something useful, Ashton, and inspect my gear instead."

Yes, Ashton, you shut up. You're a lucky one.

And luckier I certainly am. I'm the first generation born on Titan's orbital. I can't even remember anything different, only watching it on screen and thinking about my parents' nostalgic stories. Before both got killed in the quest for the perfect colony of the Solar System, martyrs of an unsung adventure. From that day on, I've become one of the halcyons, the ones that test new equipment for living on gas giants' moons. Outright suicidal, some say. But this is what I do best. And the boredom I feel at times is nothing compared to the desperation I observe in the eyes of my friends, always indoor, living like underground rodents without ever seeing daylight. Yet the longing for a planet I've never seen with my own eyes, and I belong to nevertheless, never leaves me – nor leaves them.

"Temperature check."

"Cold as usual. Make sure your isolation layer works, Leah."

"Ha-ha. I'd have already been as frozen as big blue freaking Uranus otherwise."

"Amen."

I check mine too. Lady's right, but gliding doesn't help either. As an engineer, I know that the moment we're going to launch is the most trying for materials, and I prefer having no surprises.

"Gale force check."

"Done. Winds regular and no pattern inversion for the next two weeks."

"Smashing. Possibility of rain?"

"Nope."

That's just part of the safety routine: we knew it in advance. Nobody would risk gliding on the methane seas during the wind shifts that happen twice a year: they change shape and dimensions of the sand dunes. And even less with rain, as rare as it can be. These days, everybody remains indoor. And the hell with boredom too.

"You said it before, Ashton, that's not your scene. Why have you accepted to come?"

"I've decided to give it a chance."

"I thought you were too serious for that."

"You make it sound like a contagious disease."

"Maybe it is. Your girlfriend must be worried."

"I've no girlfriend."

"Oh, you don't?"

"No. Fancy taking the risk?"

"Are you asking me out?"

"If we survive today, I might do it."

"If we survive today, I might accept."

We touch each other's hand, in that award-winning suit that leaves no room to tactile sensation. I can only imagine Leah's soft skin under my fingers. That's pleasant nonetheless. But it's a fleeting instant, and my attention is grabbed again by the view. She read me well, I do it for a living, not for entertainment. One thing wrong here, and you die. That's not my idea of fun. But if this is the only kind of fulfilment I'm able to experience, well, maybe it's the moment to change.

I admire the Vid Flumina that flows toward the sea in a beautiful estuary. Peaceful. An Earthian would mistake it for water, and try to dive in it. We know better.

She looks at me, reading my mind. I only see her eyes, but I know she's smiling. "Conditions are perfect. Let's go. Ligeia is waiting."

We strap our graphene wings onto the exoskeleton, securing their joints to its shining structure. A gust of wind blows from the East, producing a sibilant sound. Spreading our wings like weird archaeopteryx we look at the abyss and dive head down to the methane basin. Upward currents lift us for several hundred meters, before we start gliding, spiralling along in concentric circles. Then up again, in a whirling dervish dance. Our paths meet and cross while we head toward the far corners of Ligeia Mare. Saturn's rings shine in all their majesty, while the transit of Enceladus casts a round, dark shade on the sea's surface.

"Ligeia is Waiting" originally appeared in *Perihelion SF* on Wednesday, 12 April 2017

About the author

Russell Hemmell is a statistician and social scientist from the U.K, passionate about astrophysics and speculative fiction. Recent/forthcoming publications in *Aurealis, New Myths, Not One of Us,* and others. Finalist in The Caropus 100 Year Starship Awards 2016-2017.

Find her online at her blog earthianhivemind.net and on Twitter: @SPBianchini.

Oven Game

Paul A. Hamilton

The oven door creaks open, revealing the grimy, sweat-tracked face of a girl just past her seventh birthday. Opening an oven from the inside is difficult for a child, but Drea Kane has had practice. She crawls into the unfamiliar house and dusts off her black knit dress. Her grease-caked tights are living up to their name, squeezing her calves. She rubs the underside of her nose with a wrist; the streak of wetness finds its way onto her dress at the hip. The black hides the stain.

"Hello? Is anyone home?" she calls. Her voice is soft, the question more perfunctory than inquisitive. She already knows the answer.

The clock over the stovetop reads 12:34. On the other side of the oven, the time was shortly after five. She announces her presence again, bolder this time, and makes a slow turn. Drea is too young to be impressed by the kinds of details that excite home-buyers: crown moulding, hardwood floors, wide bay windows overlooking a valley bearded with evergreens. But the immensity of the house is not lost on her. The kitchen is larger than her parents' whole apartment.

She searches the house, but finds no sign of the laundry room, or of Taka. Four minutes have passed and the tights are now cutting into her feet and waist. It's happening faster this time.

It takes both hands to wrestle the tights off her legs. By the time they are clear of her calves, her shoes no longer fit. The dress is stretchy; she knows it will suffice for another few minutes, but she must find something else quickly.

Eager legs carry her out to the entryway and up the stairs, where she pauses on the broad landing. Below, the glass-inset front door glows with a sinister red shine. Every time she travels through the oven, exterior doors are blocked by the red shine. It's a barrier, because there are rules to the game. Rule number one: she cannot venture outside the homes she crawls into.

Her dress is becoming uncomfortable, the hem that once brushed the tops of her knees now barely covering her thighs. The short bob of her unruly black hair tickles past her shoulders. Rule number two: she must age quickly, like a time lapse.

There are a lot of rooms to examine. Most are grown-up rooms: a well-used study with stacks of files surrounding a computer; a library; guest rooms with empty dressers. Toward the end of the hall she finds a room that might belong to a big kid, perhaps a high schooler. Inside the large closet Drea finds three walls of thick-packed clothes on wood and metal hangers. She strips off the dress whose sleeves have drawn into tourniquets. There is a mirror behind the closet door.

She will be, according to the age acceleration provided by the oven game, a disappointingly plain teenager. Her sweet cherub cheeks will flatten into a broad face; the hugeness of her dark eyes will be overtaken by a thickening temple-to-temple slice of bushy eyebrow; her mane of hair will become an unruly thatch of kinky curls and puffy flyaways. Yet the novelty of seeing her body transform is never lost. The thick patch of moss sprouting between her legs precedes the twin bulges of her developing breasts, followed by the stretching of her legs and the outward slope of her hips. The rush of sensation from this process is difficult for her second-grade mind to grasp. A tingly exhilaration threatens to overwhelm her if she watches the transformation too long.

While she waits for her body to reach its full size, she browses the closet, thrilled again at the remarkable simplicity of being able to *reach*. Height, she has determined, is the principal joy of adulthood. She selects a pair of jeans from a shelf and pulls down a printed T-shirt. Comfortable clothes, because her body no longer provides its own comfort. She has never determined if the unease comes from invading other people's homes or from the loss of familiarity with her flesh and bones. This is her body, but during the oven game it behaves as if a new kind of gravity acts upon it.

There is a slight reluctance as she emerges from the closet. This is her favorite part of the oven game, but it always sends her belly into fluttery trembles that travel down her legs and up into her chest. She's looking for the laundry. Specifically, the dryer.

She finds the laundry room in a partitioned corner of the finished basement. She steps in and looks around. He's not here yet.

She examines her hands, remembering that while her teenage body is unremarkable, her young adult characteristics are somewhat more distinguished. The baby fat that will linger through adolescence dissipates in her early twenties. The long, lean fingers are perfect reminders of the overall sleekness that will accompany her post-collegiate years. Drea paces, worried about Taka's excessive tardiness. If her aging outstrips his, it could force her back through the oven before the rendezvous is complete. Rule number three: she must be back in the oven before old age makes the clumsy climb into the appliance impossible.

A pair of warm, smooth hands slip over her eyes and she yelps, clawing for a moment at the assailant. When his scent reaches her, raw and animal, she is reassured. She tries to spin into him, whirling her face from his cupped palms. Her shoulder catches something, hard and sharp: a shelf overhanging the laundry machines. Some of the bottles and detritus wobble and rattle together, but they settle after a tense second. Drea sighs with relief.

He laughs in her ear, a deep-voiced chuckle that sounds masculine but has the untethered emotional exuberance of a child. She grins and presses herself into his chest. Until she began playing the oven game, her father was the most handsome man alive. But this man is rugged behind a full beard instead of the careful regency of her father's thickly waxed mustaches. His hair is a rusty brown and soft, so unlike the coarse television snow of Papa's mane. And he smiles with his eyes.

Drea does not know his name. He speaks a language she doesn't understand. Often he says a word that sounds like Taka, and she has come to think of him as her Taka, though that may be his name for her. It doesn't matter. Close as she is to his breast, she can feel the tapping of his heart against hers. This is the best part of the oven game. He smiles right until the moment their lips meet. She is seven inside. Outside, she is twenty-eight, rapidly shifting into twenty-nine. This is their thirteenth kiss, and she believes Taka will be her true love forever.

"You came through early," she says when they pull away. She can't explain why her kisses with Taka are so different from her mother and father's kisses. Why they share so little in common with the goodnight pecks she gives her younger siblings on the lips before bed. An easy assumption would be that here, playing the oven game, she is different and older and therefore her kisses are more mature and sophisticated. When she daydreams, she often remembers Taka's lips.

Taka smiles and says something in his rapid, fluid tongue. Drea has learned that laughing whenever he speaks is usually the easiest way to communicate. He grins at her musical giggle and holds her out at arm's length, examining her. Taka always does this. As if watching her age is as much a part of the game for him as the kiss is for her. She notes, again, how fortunate he is to come through the dryer. Arriving in the laundry room almost always means he has ready access to clothing that will fit his expanding frame. Today he has borrowed a pair of corduroy slacks and a blue button-down which he has mis-buttoned only twice. His thickly muscled chest peeks through the open neck.

Usually, after they kiss, they hold hands and explore until they feel old and tired. At that point they separate, to return to their homes and youth. There is no fourth rule. But, if there were one, it might be this: play the game the way it is always played.

Instead, her fingers reach through the folds of the shirt to touch the skin. In thirteen expeditions through the oven, she has grown comfortable with Taka. Her action is tender; anything but aggressive. Perhaps it is merely the unexpected sensation, or that Drea changes the game, unchanged for months, spontaneously.

Whatever the cause, Taka recoils from her touch. His movements remind Drea of a marionette whose paddle is shaken in frustration. He leaps back, pressing himself clumsily against the wall.

"I'm sorry," Drea begins, but she is interrupted by a tremendous crash. The bracket her shoulder hit moments before rips free of the wall. It might have fallen anyway. The shelf is overloaded with the sorts of household items that don't typically have a comfortable home: heavy bottles of bleach, stain-fighting solvents, cans of touch-up paint for the upstairs bedrooms. It could have been seconds from falling already. The impact of Taka's back on the wall could have sent it crashing down either way. But as Drea watches the slow yet inexorable chain reaction play out, she can't stop remembering: she bumped it first.

The contents of the shelf topple and fall half a meter onto the dryer's flat metal top. Jugs and canisters bash into the top of the dryer with a series of deafening metallic clangs. Taka and Drea clap their hands over their ears in helpless fascination, watching the rain of miscellaneous items batter and dent the lint-coated surface of the appliance.

At last a small fabric softener ball rolls off the crooked shelf. It bounces, almost cheerful, from the warped dryer top to the pile of broken and leaking cans and bottles on the floor. The smell of mixing chemicals stings their eyes and noses, and they turn worried expressions toward each other. They have always been careful not to leave evidence behind when playing the oven game. No one has ever been home, but the houses always seem lived in, never abandoned. Drea consistently battles the fear of being caught. This terrible mess will be impossible to clean before they are too old to manage a mop or broom any longer.

She hears a choking sound come from Taka, like a sob.

"What's wrong?" she asks. Taka moves closer to the dryer, staring at the pull-down handle on the door. The metal has crumpled, obstructing the door. An icy breeze whispers along her back. Neither of them moves for a long moment until Drea looks up and sees small sparkles of white snow through his hair.

"Can you open it?"

Taka presses his lips together, understanding enough to know he has to try. There's no use staring, wishing it undone.

As soon as it's obvious Taka can barely curl his fingers under the beaten metal to grasp the handle, Drea knows it will not open. Taka yanks, and the whole dryer screeches forward across the dirty tile, but the door holds fast. He says something vulgar-sounding through gritted teeth and bashes the door furiously. The appliance becomes wild in its rocking, its plastic-coated feet beating against the floor. Taka's frenzied effort fills the basement with deafening, overlapping echoes.

"Stop! Stop!" Drea screams over the racket. "That's not helping." She tries to think, but Taka is panicking, the sweat and tears mixing into a salty shine on his face. Crow's feet collect the squeezed tears and run them to the outside of his beautiful cheeks.

With a jerky motion, Drea grabs Taka's hand. "Come on," she says, pulling Taka toward the kitchen. She never considered what might happen if they played the game until they couldn't escape. When she first discovered the secret door at the back of her parents' oven, she stayed for hours. Then she found the delightful stoop of her spine and the charming thinness of her legs nearly stopped her from crawling back. But as long as she could make it into the oven, she emerged in her parents' apartment the same age as when she left, only a few seconds having passed.

She knows Taka might not get home right away if he can't go back through the dryer. But if she can get him to her house, maybe they will be able to return tomorrow or in a couple of days. Or he could try a different dryer. There are many questions unanswered, and a lot of unknowns, but she is certain they can't stay. Eventually Taka will get too old to leave at all. She doesn't like thinking what that might mean. A quiet but insistent corner of her mind worries it could signal the end of the oven game.

She examines the kitchen before making any moves toward the stove. No overhanging shelves, only a large hood built right into the wall. It seems unlikely it could crash down and block their second escape, too.

But she hadn't considered the laundry shelf a threat, either.

Unlike Taka, Drea always leaves the oven doors open behind her. She's irrationally annoyed that he did not have the foresight to take this small precaution. She gestures at the oven and catches a look of deep-creased worry on Taka's face. He is aging even more rapidly than usual. They both have been, she knows. Frustrated by his hesitation, Drea pushes him toward the portal.

"Go! Climb in," she says.

Taka looks terrified, but flashes Drea a weak, thankful smile before putting his hands onto the lowered door and crawling in. She notices for the first time that ovens in the game have their racks lowered, almost to the elements. This strikes her as unusual, but she doesn't have time to ponder it further. Her breath catches and she waits for him to disappear.

His head vanishes into the darkness of the oven. A moment later she hears a light thump followed by a small whimper of pain as Taka runs head first into the rear of the stove.

"No," Drea says in exasperation, reaching out to pull him back by the seat of his corduroys, "you have to open the little slide-door first! Don't you know anything?" Taka rolls aside and Drea leans on the oven door. It groans under the weight of the two adults. She gropes in the claustrophobic dark for the tiny handle, the one that allows her to move into the oven game.

The handle isn't there.

"That's impossible," she says. "Here, get off." She makes way, noting a new twinge of discomfort in her middle back. Taka groans his way off the oven door and Drea crawls in as quickly as her stooping bones will allow. Alone now, she finds the handle right away. She slides the panel open and sees her own parents' kitchen.

"There!" she cries, and wriggles backward, leaving the passage open for Taka to use. She turns to him, seeing a smear of ashy grease on his forehead. He squats, a mixture of pain from his bulging knees and deep concern in his eyes. "Look," Drea says, "you can go now." He looks in bewilderment at the oven's interior and shakes his head. "Go!" Drea practically screams at him.

With reluctance, Taka pulls himself into the oven again and pauses just before the open passage. "Well go on," Drea says, exasperated. Taka looks over his thinning shoulder. His hand reaches out toward the dim light of her home. It stops, meeting obvious but invisible resistance. He feels along the empty space between the oven game and her home, like a mime with a vein-splintered hand. He turns to her, questioning.

"No," Drea says. It is the only word she can remember. No. No. No. This cannot be. She pulls him out again and crawls in, ignoring the curl of her own aging fingers as they push through the charred crumbs at the bottom of the strangers' oven cavity. Her face passes the barrier that blocked Taka, but she's careful not to go all the way through. She smells the familiar sandalwood and cinnamon aroma of home. The passage works. She scoots free and stands, reaching around to clutch her back against the hurry of her spine's curve.

"You can make it," she pleads, "you have to."

Taka shakes his head. He says something quiet. He sounds resigned. His beard is white. His hair is snowy. His eyes are sad but kind.

"You have to!" Drea screams at him. "You have to!" She cries. "You can't stay here. You just can't."

Taka reaches out to her, pulls her into a hug. He whispers. She doesn't know the words, but she understands completely. Her hips ache. Her eyes blur, even beyond the mist of the tears she can't stop. He doesn't kiss her one last time. Instead, he rubs his thumbs along her cheeks so her vision clears momentarily, and then he nods toward the open stove. His own atrophying muscles offer what little help they can. Drea hesitates in her crawl, turning back. He puts a hand on the small of her back, urging her forward.

When the oven door slams closed in her kitchen, she turns a seven year-old head and peers through the opening. She needs Taka to know she's coming back for him. Sometimes it takes a day or two, sometimes weeks before the oven is ready for her to play again, but she is impatient this time. She needs to return right away, with her youth reset. She needs to try to save him again.

She sees nothing. Just the dark gray back of a cold appliance she shouldn't be playing with in the first place.

She never plays the oven game again, though she tries to daily, even hourly at first, for months. Her parents are concerned. She cries herself to sleep and says disturbing things about her imaginary friend, Taka, who has apparently aged himself to death somehow. They send her to therapy.

After some time, Drea claims it is helping. She stops talking about Taka, but the dreams take longer to fade.

As a plain teenager, desperate for acceptance, she tells a new friend about the Oven Game, in confidence. The look on the other girl's face is stricken and horrified.

"You're sick," the girl says. "Why would you make up something like that?"

Drea can't answer. She struggles to remember which parts of the Oven Game were real and which were dreams.

In the casually cruel manner of teens, Drea is quickly branded a freak; a weirdo who lies to get attention. She goes back to being friendless, and sobs to her therapist, "I just want to stop dreaming about these stories!"

"It's good that you refer to those events as stories. I'm glad to hear you frame them as made-up," her therapist says in that soft, non-confrontational way of psychiatrists.

"But the dreams," Drea says miserably.

Her therapist taps a pen to her lips. "Have you ever tried hypnosis?" she asks. Drea sits up a little straighter and wipes her eyes.

By the time Drea graduates from high school, she sleeps soundly at last. Memories of her childhood playtimes fade, like polaroid photos tossed into an old shoebox.

Drea is a capable woman, just past her thirty-sixth birthday. She has two teenage children and a busy husband, plus an accounting job she loves. Her life is extraordinarily normal, and she tells this to people at her simple yet elegant cocktail parties with a self-deprecating laugh.

Even her husband, Trey, doesn't know about the troubles she went through as a young girl with an overactive imagination who frightened parents, teachers, and classmates with elaborate stories. She has worked very hard for over twenty years to ignore her life before college. When she thinks back to her childhood, which is very rarely, it feels as if it were something she read in a book. Those years happened to someone else, and the memories are hazy and slippery, which doesn't bother her in the least.

Everyone believes she is completely normal, and that makes her very happy.

Trey and Drea have moved around a lot. Trey's job requires frequent relocation, and Drea has been game to start over on many occasions. Re-establishing herself at a new job and settling the kids into new schools is always the hardest; even that has become somewhat routine. Her favorite part is house-hunting. They've bought or rented many places over the years and Drea has always been the one to make the final decision. Trey likes to joke about Drea's "house feelings:" they never choose a home unless Drea walks through and declares, "Yep, this feels right." She can't explain the house feelings. Some places, when she walks in, just make her happy, a sensation she says is like a cozy fire and hot tea on a winter night.

But now they have their dream house at last, a gorgeous near-mansion overlooking a valley in the Colorado hills. She has found a position that suits her with a company she likes. The kids have made fast friends at school. Trey loves the proximity to the ski slopes and the grandeur of the kitchen, which has always been his domain. Drea hates to cook.

Because of all this, they worry about the next transfer, even if it may be years away. She doesn't want to leave a place where everything is perfect.

Almost perfect. Lately, she has noticed some peculiar occurrences. Break-ins, she thinks. It started a dozen or so moves ago, and it seems to have become more common. They are almost, but not quite, predictable with each new home. From time to time the family will be away for a day or an afternoon and come home to the distinct impression that someone has been in their house. Nothing valuable is ever stolen, the door and window alarms are never tripped. But the eerie sense of ghostly presences is palpable.

Drea would dismiss these notions if her husband and the kids didn't remark on them. There are small evidences of invasion: a tiny sock; clothing missing from her son's room; an unused closet door left ajar; a smear of a handprint on a doorframe, far too small and low to the ground to belong to her teenaged children.

This morning, she comes home from an overnight business trip and enters the kitchen. She lets out a single, unbroken scream that causes the neighbors to call the police.

When the responding team arrives, they enter the kitchen where a woman stands over the bones of an elderly man. She is shrieking, weeping and inconsolable. The only sign of struggle is rooms away, in the basement. The laundry area is wrecked. A shelf has broken, its contents scattered on the floor. The dryer is damaged, its door bent and stuck fast.

The woman cannot be persuaded to say anything other than a single word, over and over and over: "Taka."

"Oven Game" originally appeared in *Metaphorosis*
on Friday, 18 August 2017

About the author

Paul A. Hamilton is a writer, editor, and technologist living in Northern California with his wife and two daughters. His stories feature broken people, reassembled worlds, beautiful monsters, and hideous love. He gets his inspiration by impersonating an old-timey bartender, listening to stories told by lonely strangers. When not writing, he can be found reading. drawing, taking photographs, or riding roller coasters.

More from him can be found at ironsoap.com, and @ironsoap.

Cold Comforts

Graham Robert Scott

In the recording, the audio kicks in before the video does. Hera hears her son's voice in the background.

"Start a proxy," he says.

She detects a slight tremble, hints of resignation and sorrow. His face appears on the screen then. Haggard, bristly. Rings under brown eyes.

"Who would you like to proxy?" the ship intelligence replies.

"Mum," his voice says with a crack. "Dad."

"Oh, Leo," she says to the screen in her booth. He cannot hear her. He is, or was, almost 3 billion miles away. Which means he hasn't yet heard about his father. Doesn't know his father will never view this message. At current distances, each message takes more than a week to reach its destination.

In the recording, however, it's only a second before the pseudo-intelligent proxies engage.

"Leo!" her own voice says on the recording, incongruously upbeat. "What a pleasant surprise!"

"Hey, champ," says her husband's proxy.

"Uh, hey Mum. Dad," Leo replies.

With the proxies, her son has always been awkward, an ironically poor imitation of himself. He pauses, unable to make eye contact with the camera.

"Son?" her husband's proxy says. "Are you okay?"

Hera sees the slight shake of Leo's head. *No. Obviously, he isn't.* The proxy version of her, however, misses the cue.

"Did you get our Christmas videos?" the imitation asks.

Insensitive bitch, Hera thinks.

He nods, distracted. "I have some bad news."

There's a strangled, pained, anticipatory sound from the simulated mother. It's a sound of dread and suspense, and uncannily accurate, for the real mother in her booth realizes she made the same sound days ago.

Leo sniffs, long and wet, runs a hand through untamed hair.

"The Graff manoeuvre didn't work."

Proxy Mum gasps. Proxy Dad is barely audible as a low moan.

"But ... That can't be," she hears her voice saying.

Leo waits for it to sink in.

"They were so sure!" her voice says. "They said it was a near certainty!"

"Those bastards," her husband's voice grumbles. "I warned them. They dismissed me as out of touch with the latest figures and I bought it. Those cocky bastards."

"I know it's a surprise," Leo says. "I'm a bit ... stunned, too. The odds of failure were low. But they're always there. You know that, Dad."

Proxy Dad says nothing.

"So now what? What's the next step?" her distant voice asks, although the listening mother already knows, had already figured it out from the looks she got as they led her to the booth, and from her husband's death at his own hand, five days earlier, amid pictures of Leo and a storm of scribbled equations.

Leo takes a deep breath. "There isn't one, Mum. I'm not coming home," he says.

The Proxy Mum erupts into shuddering sobs, and the listening mother is disoriented to hear the soundtrack of her soul while her own throat squeezes out almost no sound at all.

Since he sent this message, he's already died, Hera realizes. How did it happen? Did he drift ever lower until crushed and irradiated? Did he find a better way to die?

Proxy Mum has the same question. Or a version of it.

"Wh — what are you going to do?"

"Keep working. Until I can't."

Proxy Dad intrudes: "To hell with that. Don't suffer. Take the pill."

At this, Hera chokes on an involuntary sound, halfway between a sob and a growl. Lacking a pill, her husband had taken a bullet.

"We lost automation in the earlier collision," her son explains. "The only way we're going to get data on the way down is if I run the show by hand."

"So — what? You're going to be *awake as you're crushed?*" her voice protests.

"I'll take the pill when it's too much to bear."

Her proxy voice is quiet, feeble, when it answers: "But I don't want you to reach that point."

"It's another two minutes after you take it," adds the unsteady voice of Leo's father.

"I know," Leo says.

And then he sits there. His posture reminds the listening mother of times in his childhood when they sat him at the kitchen table, after he had admitted to wrongdoing. It's his Awaiting Judgement Slouch.

Her proxy picks up on it, too.

"I'm so sorry, son," Proxy Mum says. Her voice wavers at first, then strengthens, as if she's summoned the courage to reassure. "We are going to miss you very, very much."

"I miss you already," Leo mumbles.

"I know we resisted your ambitions at first," her proxy continues. "But we are so proud of you. Your accomplishments. Your bravery."

Leo cries.

"You're the best thing that ever happened to me," says her dead husband's voice. "I couldn't have asked for a better son."

Leo sobs.

"I've gotta go," Leo sniffs. "Thank you for ... well, everything. I love you, both of you, more than I know how to articulate. And I'm so, so sorry."

He disconnects. The light of the screen winks out, replaced by a dull, flickering grey that isn't quite black, and the booth goes dark.

Leo's widowed mother sits alone. On her end, there is no proxy son.

Outside the booth, 18 people pretend to work. None looks at the booth, but all listen. For a minute, there's silence from the widow and mother inside. Then screaming. Enraged invective and profanity. Employees exchange awkward glances, but no one moves towards the door.

Eventually, someone has to talk to the woman. To a woman who just listened as a ship took her place during her child's last moments, far from home.

But no one wants to be first.

"Cold Comforts" originally appeared in *Nature* on Thursday, 6 April 2017

About the author

Graham Robert Scott has published stories in *Nature* and in *Barrelhouse Online*. An English professor at Texas Woman's University and former journalist, he writes nonfiction under the byline Gray Scott.

Graham can be followed on Twitter @graythebruce, and on his blog at hemicyon.blogspot.com.

Lake Oreyd

Damien Krsteski

The lake's still surface was a golden quilt. The churches which amassed along the shore over the centuries now had their fossilized features balanced between day and night. A most sacred moment. The eyestalks, V-shaped like the chalice from which the Savior had drunk her poison, framed the setting sun, the tails like the scepters with which she'd been prodded to trial facing the rising moon.

One intake of breath, the sun dipped down, pulling the moon up, and the alignment was broken.

The podvodnya sank; my ears popped as we descended, and looking out the thick, round window it seemed as if the lake's waters darkened in hue with each blink of the eye. When we neared the bottom some hours later, all was pitch black. The vessel's searchlight turned on to sweep below us.

Corroded broken pipes lay in the sediment, barnacled and covered with algae. Our podvodnya crawled the lake's bottom, much like benthic creatures of the past must have when they sought the source of God, tentacles sifting through silt, clawing at mud, chasing away eels which sparkled in the dark.

We could see only within that circle of pale light: our window to His underwater Kingdom.

TAPE A/0; ARCHIVED

Q: [garbled]

A: Woolsbnick College. On the first, second, and fourth expedition. I was slated to join the last one, too, but certain *academic* obligations kept me from doing so. Fortunately, as it turned out.

Q: [garbled]

A: Ah, apologies. Professor Vyktor Claude.

Q: [garbled]

Prof. Claude: That's a very personal question.

Q: [garbled]

Prof. Claude: Yes, I suppose it is relevant. Well. Why couldn't one believe in both? I've spent my entire life—not just academic life, mind you—reconciling my faith with science. And while it hasn't always been straightforward, I believe I've managed quite well thus far. My work in academia is an extension of my beliefs, you see, a study of the color and shape of the individual tiles making up our Universe. Science is the details. But then I pull back, and admire the mosaic. And that's my faith. So, yes, both.

Q: [garbled]

Prof. Claude: No, I don't think that makes me biased. I'm an academic first and foremost.

Q: [garbled]

Prof. Claude: It was a tragedy. I lost brothers and sisters down there, and it's an insult to their memory to so casually dismiss the expeditions as unsuccessful. One must look beyond the official records, peel away the dry facts on the surface to realize we didn't altogether fail to find something. Perhaps we failed to *define* that something. But down there we knew, may the Savior bless the souls of those now gone, we knew we felt it. Certainly those of us unblinded by bitter skepticism did. I kept a journal of my research which I may someday publish, primarily as a counterweight to that bland report released by the College, and perhaps people will accept the truth then.

Q: [garbled]

Prof. Claude: It's difficult to describe to somebody so obviously skeptical.

Q: [garbled]

Prof. Claude: You're right. I'm not here to disabuse you of your notions. [sighing] A presence. That's the simplest way to describe the feeling, even though that particular word, loaded and full of connotation, a cliché, really, doesn't do it justice. And before you even bring it up, yes, I do take into account underwater pressure, dizziness, claustrophobia, low levels of oxygen, anxiety, the hypnotic effect of the drone of the podvodnya sonar exacerbated by the syncing of our breathing. All those figure into the equation, as it were, and I still end up with the conviction that the particular presence we— that *I* felt, was a physical manifestation, and not something imagined, conjured out of fantasy.

Q: [garbled]

Prof. Claude: Glad to, but first, may I have a glass of tap water?

TAPE B/0; ARCHIVED

Q: [garbled]

A: Helmsman Petr, sir. I piloted the podvodnya on two of the five dives.

Q: [garbled]

Petr: Only as a replacement for the Master Helmsman, may the Savior cradle his soul in Her arms.

Q: [garbled]

Petr: Descent number two and descent number three.

Q: [garbled]

Petr: No, sir, didn't pay them much mind, truth be told. They had their faces stuck to the windows, fogging 'em up with their breath, and they scratched notes in their little pads. My eyes were on the path ahead. Hands never leaving the control levers.

Q: [garbled]

Petr: Like I said, mainly quiet. As you'd expect from learned types, professors.

Q: [garbled]

Petr: Sheets of rusted metal from old sunken vessels, broken pipes of sewage, silt, mud, the occasional fish here and there. I've been to the bottom dozens of times when training with the Master, and these two descents with the scholars weren't any different, I can assure you.

Q: [garbled]

Petr: Why, of course, sir. I loved him like a father. [pause] More than an employer, he was my mentor. [pause] And to think how much I still had to learn from him...

Q: [garbled]

Petr: That's all right. Thank you.

Q: [garbled]

Petr: No, we never spoke of clients, that'd be unprofessional. They weren't more than cargo to us, if you see what I mean. We pilot our vessel, we take passengers down, bring them back up. All there is to it. The Master never spoke of what went on in the podvodnya, and neither did I. At the end of the day, we got paid, that's all that mattered to us, that we'd a hot meal on our table.

Q: [garbled]

Petr: Of course. Will try, sir.

Fish swam into view in our light cone. Each a miracle of life, a proof of the versatility of the Creator and His blessed agile hands, but also a gift from this world to our Savior, the holy daughter who sacrificed Herself so we can enjoy our lives here.

The tentacles of the podvodnya cleared away corroded debris from our path. The boy helmsman, wet behind the ears but utterly focused on the task at hand, started when I put my hand on his shoulder.

"Here," I said, my finger on the topographical map of the lake's bottom. "We should be in this section by now. We can pause here."

He shot me a sidelong glance, as if questioning the gall of my dishing out orders in his vessel, then he blinked, and his expression was that of a naïve child again. "Of course, sir."

The area was part of a bay around which many of those gigantic molluscs had gathered to slake their thirst. I gazed into the dark waters, enthralled. Innards grumbling, the podvodnya crawled to a stop. I recited a short prayer (my two colleagues indulging me with silence) and pulled the plunger set into the curved wall of the pod, slowly drawing out the one liter of water from the lake I needed for studies.

The boy watched us intently while my colleagues fiddled with their instruments, performing their own studies, and while I marveled at the murky view.

When we surfaced, we emerged from one darkness only to plunge into another: night had fallen, and starlight rippled around the buoyed vessel. The boy helmsman switched off the main engine, and popped the top-hatch; I climbed half-way out of it to help paddle to shore. As if sailing over the heavens themselves, I was rearranging constellations with each dip of my oar.

On the shingled beach, the boy started to service his podvodnya, and my colleagues broke into a livid discussion on the aquatic life—and incongruity thereof— we'd just witnessed. Quietly, I walked up to one of the churches, preserved forever perched with its beak dipped in the lake.

Its mother-of-pearl shell was coated with creamy starlight, the preserved ommatophores sticking out of it. I caressed the hollow shell with the tips of my fingers. I could sense the thrum of the wind inside it. The tremor spread into my hand, arm, torso, and legs, and my knees buckled. I crawled through the opening into the shell of the animal, into holy ground, and prayed in whispers.

TAPE C/0; ARCHIVED

Q: [garbled]

A: Professor Perevana, Woolsbnick College, Department of Natural Sciences.

Q: [garbled]

Prof. Perevana: I joined the rotating cast of researchers from Woolsbnick, once. Went down on the very first expedition. The helmsman was a burly, bearded man. Poor soul.

Q: [garbled]

Prof. Perevana: I don't think I recall—oh, you refer to the helmsman's apprentice, perhaps? Now that you brought it up, I do remember a young boy milling around at the dock.

Q: [garbled]

Prof. Perevana: Once proved enough for me.

Q: [garbled]

Prof. Perevana: Because God is not to be found lurking in the depths of some lake. There's nothing there but mud and rusted iron.

Q: [garbled]

Prof. Perevana: My colleague's *theories*? No, I've heard no *theorizing* from him, I'm sorry to say, only posturing. He's a blowhard interested only in himself, his own fame and fortune.

Q: [garbled]

Prof. Perevana: Wasn't I clear enough? Of course I don't believe him. Neither him nor any of the other endemic-religiosity quote-unquote researchers. I've been opposing Oreyd creationist myths my entire career. That's why I signed up for this expedition, why I went down. To shut those nutters up once and for all, to have an ace up my sleeve: *Yes, I went down there, and saw nothing preternatural, and nothing was unearthed, and nothing ever will be.* The skeptics are always right, remember that. Professor Claude is a clown with an agenda.

Q: [garbled]

Prof. Perevana: Feel free to leaf through my section of the official Woolsbnick report.

TAPE A/1; ARCHIVED

Q: [garbled]

Prof. Claude: Yes, let's talk about the churches. [sipping water]

Q: [garbled]

Prof. Claude: I'm sorry but I see no contradiction. Like I said before, I am a scholar first, conciliator of faith and science second. I accept scientific findings, and see how they can be superimposed over my view of the world. Fit into the mosaic, to return to my earlier analogy. So, I say the fact these churches are of biological origin does not make them any less divine. Those creatures, whose anatomy resembles our most holy of symbols, were drawn to Lake Oreyd, miles away from the southern mangroves, despite an abundance of drinking water from lakes and rivers near their initial habitat. No one in their right mind can chalk that up to chance; it took me a while to understand, but it was a pilgrimage, pure and simple.

Q: [garbled]

Prof. Claude: Papers have been published claiming either way. But based on recent fossil dating techniques, these creatures lived around 255 S. E. The first symbols of our faith had already appeared—see the great archaeological work of Professors Swolia and Alynia, around Mynistiris—circa 100 S. E., so the chalices and the rulers' scepters appeared some 150 years prior, before our race had even set foot near any of these creatures' habitats.

Q: [garbled]

Prof. Claude: Absolutely. A simultaneous appearance of our Creator's symbols in our world, half a continent apart.

Q: [garbled]

Prof. Claude: There seems to be a certain connection between us, these creature-churches, and the lake. A symbiosis. It is my belief the link *itself* is of divine nature, yet another intricate puzzle our Creator has set up for us to attempt to solve. We always try these puzzles, and always end up with a small but crucial piece missing.

Q: [garbled]

Prof. Claude: No, I see that as the Creator's sense of humor. [laughter] A way to show us there still remains joy in this world.

TAPE C/1; ARCHIVED

Prof. Perevana: Humans have imitated nature since time immemorial, we derive symbols from natural occurrences, recognize patterns where there are none. The quote-unquote churches are the remains of an extinct species (*nautilus giganteus superior*) that used to feed in the lake, most probably on the endemic trout (*salmo letnica*), now also extinct. Our ancestors must have been drawn to these magnificent shells, and their fossilized eyestalks and tails, and fashioned religious symbols out of them.

Q: [garbled]

Prof. Perevana: Many species migrate for one reason or another. These creatures might have shared the fertile land around Mynistiris with the early human settlers before being driven away by hunters; or humans might have traveled south to explore warmer climates and encountered the beasts there. In my opinion there's a higher probability of beasts and humans coexisting long enough for early hominids to derive religious symbols from the animals' appearance, than this ridiculous story of spontaneous manifestation of the Creator.

Q: [garbled]

Prof. Perevana: Yes, probability, possibility, *may* be, *could* be. That's the key difference. Our camp avoids speaking in absolutes.

Laboratory examinations of the lake's water proved inconclusive. Apart from plankton already studied and cataloged by scholars fifty years before, no further microscopic life was found. Could there exist life even more minuscule than what our apparatus can see? Or should I discard biology altogether, and trust my instinct, my belief that this water itself is of divine provenance, regardless of what microbiota swirl within it?

No, my belief is my belief, but it won't silence the skeptics. Further experiments need to be performed.

Electrolysis, and spectroscopy, and its effect on physical materials, and administration to living tissue.

TAPE B/1; ARCHIVED

Q: [garbled]

Petr: Thank you. Good to see you too, sir.

Q: [garbled]

Petr: Yes, I suppose that's how these things happen. Out of grief, I'd just ... didn't want to think...

Q: [garbled]

Petr: Some water would be great.

Q: [garbled]

Petr: The other day I was at the cabin by the lake, you know, from where we ran our business. Went through the equipment, checking, re-checking ropes, pipes, pulleys and levers, the diving logs again—

Q: [garbled]

Petr: No, everything was in its place. It's just— holding the Master's tools again, his pencil, his yellow scratch-pad diving log, it made—it made me remember things that'd slipped my mind, sir. I mean, truth be told, I don't know whether it's important, or relevant to your investigation, but last time you said to let you know if anything came back. Anything whatsoever. Regardless of how unconnected it might seem. Well, holding my Master's tools like so, I remembered the night before the last dive. [pause] How he was up all night.

Q: [garbled]

Petr: The night prior to, yes. Which was unusual, he always slept soundly. I sleep in the room next to his, and on this night, I remember hearing his bed creaking as he'd get up and then lie back down, hearing him pace his room, open and close desk drawers, the clinking of tools, even. They woke me up throughout the night, those sounds coming from his room, but I'd cover my head with the pillow, each time, and go back to sleep.

Q: [garbled]

Petr: No, just in his room.

Q: [garbled]

Petr: The vessel seemed to be in good condition. So far as I know. Normally, I help him check it myself before each dive. Another pair of eyes, he always said.

But this morning he seemed uninterested in my assistance. I did a sort of cursory glance inspection, so to speak. Then he said everything was all right, I'd better get back to cleaning the storeroom.

Q: [garbled]

Petr: I know it's not much, but you said anything, and this came to mind...

Q: [garbled]

Petr: Well, who knows? I'm going to take a breather, first. Clear out my head. But then, I suppose, I'm going to keep running the shop. I owe it to the Master's memory, if nothing else.

I held the last drops of the lake sample in a vial in my hand. Pale blue water swirled in it, a piece of the depths, of the dark of the lake now brought to light in my laboratory. In my hand.

Into my pocket.

I hurried home.

Enough of this. The machines have declared no difference exists between holy water and what comes out the faucet, but that's to be expected, because machines don't have the eyes to see the Creator.

One more crucial test remains, a test whose results cannot be jotted down in numeric symbols. The test of subjectivity.

TAPE A/2; ARCHIVED

Q: [garbled]

Prof. Claude: Well, she can insult me as much as she wishes, but same goes for her, don't you think? Milla Perevana built a career out of trying to dismantle our arguments. She, too, has something at stake. She's not the impartial observer she portrays herself as.

Q: [garbled]

Prof. Claude: No, we avoid each other skillfully at Woolsbnick. Our paths cross only in scholarly journals, taking shots at one another from opposite thematic sections. [laughter]

Q: [garbled]

Prof. Claude: Yes, let's go back to that.

Q: [garbled]

Prof. Claude: Well, tell me, have you ever set foot in one?

Q: [garbled]

Prof. Claude: There's a hum that envelops you, and you sit down in the middle of the shell, breathe in, breathe out. You can hear your pulse. But gradually, as you calm down, the hum becomes a whisper, morphing into a speech consisting of your inner thoughts, and you breathe in, breathe out, and listen to what you're thinking. The Creator speaks to you, through you, then. It's a beautiful experience. You learn about yourself.

Q: [garbled]

Prof. Claude: That I feel... Look. Can I tell you a story? Tape won't run out? All right. When I first started going to church, one particular memory seemed to resonate in that shell. When I was a kid my mother would sometimes read to me at bedtime from this book, *Stories from the City in the Mirror*. Not often, but some nights. Nights when my grandfather was out and it was late and we wanted to keep each other company. We wouldn't speak of him: I never asked where he was, she pretended not to care. It was our ritual. She'd read, I'd listen, and we'd try not to think of what would happen when he returned. One particularly rainy night, she read to me, and I remember the drone of her voice—I could hear it in the hum of the church—and the rain lashing against my bedroom window as if in waves, at the mercy of the wind. From the hallway came the sound of key turning in lock, of our heavy oak door opening—being thrown open—before slamming shut. A tremor passed through the walls. My mother stopped reading to listen to her father's footsteps, mentally charting his stumble through the house. When the footsteps neared my bedroom, she shut the book, and got out. Throughout the clamor that ensued I had my eyes glued to my little bedroom window, at the pale starlight smeared onto the pane by blotches of rain. A while later, she returned. I tried not to look at her face. She placed the book in her lap again, and picked up the story where she'd left off. Growing up, I've been telling myself stories were her way of getting away from everything, keeping his looming presence and the crushing agony of our poverty out of her mind. Childishly protected, almost, in that fairytale bubble we shared. But the Creator's voice, distinct in the hum in His church, made me reconsider my interpretation of events, and memories returned to me of her focus, her verve, the cadence of her reading voice. No, it wasn't a perfunctory act. To say her reading was an escape would demean the act. She was there because she felt an obligation to the stories, an obligation magnified by those bursts of unkindness of which she'd been on the receiving end her whole life, and storytelling was *really* sacred to her, one of the last sacred things, a way to preserve some kind of balance. She must've believed what I myself believe now, that all stories are windows into one big, eternal Story, a Story that screams to be told, even to a frightened, bedwetting child who wouldn't remember a single word come morning.

Q: [garbled]

Prof. Claude: When you're told a story, you experience a created world, a world in which everything has purpose. Characters say words for a reason, sunbeams caress the faces of pretty women, kings rule over kingdoms, and peasants revolt; there exists a beginning, a middle, an end. A plot drives the actions of the protagonists of the tales; there is a reason for the telling, a moral to be derived at the end. When one believes in the Creator, one applies those same principles to this world we inhabit. Every individual moment happens because it's been slated to happen, every monad is placed where it ought to be. Our world has a beginning, a middle, an end. It has a plot, and a reason for being.

Q: [garbled]

Prof. Claude: Life means something, don't you agree?

I am sitting on the beach. I write this as it happens. Important details could be lost, and it's crucial I note down everything.

I drank the water less than an hour ago. When I did, I felt like vomiting, but I chalk that up to nerves. It tasted fresh, still cold. I felt as if drinking our Creator's essence.

The sky won't give up its darkness. The lake is calm, ready to accept us once again into its depths. Dawn is moments away. The city still sleeps behind the hill.

I sit, and wait.

TAPE C/2; ARCHIVED

Q: [garbled]

Prof. Perevana: One could easily whip oneself into a frenzy, especially if one has the predilection to believe in one's own mysticism.

Q: [garbled]

Prof. Perevana: Papers have been published by colleagues of mine, which you can read through, studying the so-called *self-delusion effect:* it appears in children who've suffered trauma, supplanting painful childhood memories with made-up stories; in dying patients who see visions of dead relatives; in sleep-deprived people hallucinating scenarios where they—

Q: [garbled]

Prof. Perevana: Point being, *seeing* things, *having visions,* is not medically mysterious. It's quite common. Keep in mind, the subject might be dead certain the hallucinated events had transpired—they might not necessarily be lying.

Q: [garbled]

Prof. Perevana: I'm not accusing anybody of anything. Citing research is all I'm doing.

Q: [garbled]

Prof. Perevana: Look. [pause] Understand, it's far from innocuous what they're doing, diverting precious College funds from vital research and into expeditions to prove their ... *fantasy.* There's nothing personal here.

Q: [garbled]

Prof. Perevana: Not necessarily *my* research, but more important, scholarly work. Lives could be saved if those funds are funneled into, say, medical studies.

Black gives way to violet gives way to blue. The lake's surface brightens, reminding me of that emergence from the depths, that coming back into the world. The lake is a womb, our each resurfacing a rebirth.

A light breeze picks up.

The churches around me glimmer with the light of a sun still unseen. Their nacreous shells catch color. Catch the first rays of sunshine, as the sun quietly rises.

I breathe slowly, contemplating my work. Tingling in my legs. Like spiders crawling all over my skin. Tingling becomes a burst of electricity that grips me. Excitement courses through me, and I begin to laugh, laughing hard and loud, because I realize—how stupid I'd been to think otherwise—I realize the machines were right all along.

Yes, there is no difference between faucet and lake water. Of course. They are both one and the same—holy water, touched by our Creator, drunk by our Savior, by all of us.

The world is starting to spin around me. Waves on the lake. Surf, nibbling on the shingled shore. The ground beneath me gives way, I feel unsteady, as if on a buoy.

These churches, creatures, their thirst for this lake's water was a pilgrimage, not for the contents of what they'd lapped up on these shores, but because every step is a pilgrimage and every movement a celebration of life. All of us, searching, we're nothing but pilgrims.

A noise. From further down the beach. The cabin.

Clanging of metal. Voices. The sky is radiant with light and I'm sprawled on my back.

I'm dizzy. It's hard to write. But I must. I will.

The voices, a noise two-fold. Two figures on the shore. They're gauzy shadows. Can't make them out. They're talking. God and Goddess.

Creator, show me what my eyes ought to see, whisper to me what my ears must hear. The world spins faster.

I get up and hide behind a church. My heart is racing.

My hand trembles when I hold the pencil. Must not pause. I press my cheek against the cold hard shell of the church, and it soothes me.

God and His Daughter, the Creator and the Savior, caressing the podvodnya, blessing it with their touch. I just threw up. Nerves, getting worse. Hard to see. Harder to hear. Surf, wind, pulse pounding in my ears. Must focus and write.

They don't notice me watching them.

Home. Decided to go home.

I stumble homeward, making brief pauses to catch my breath, throw up, and write this down. The world's no longer spinning as much.

In my home now after a long walk. A quiet apartment, no humming.

Welcoming this new day drained, empty of fluids. Calmer. My body has expelled all skepticism. Exhausted. Must sleep now.

Will write more tomorrow. Am shaking.

The Creator has spared me. There's nothing more to it.

I was trembling in my blanket in the afternoon when Professor Colym came to see me. He was relieved to the point of tears I was there, sick in my house, and not on the expedition. He informed me of the accident.

They'd just dredged it out, he said, the podvodnya. Crushed from the pressure like a tin can under a boulder. A crack on the outer hull, some overlooked structural weakness, the politsiya had relayed to Colym. Their bodies ruined, a paste of bone and gore. The merry faces of our colleagues came to me, and we both cried for them.

When he left I stopped crying. I was confused. The beach, the shapes on the beach, my vision. The Creator and the Savior took care of me.

They'd taken those poor souls in Their embrace, but chased me away from the beach, keeping me away from that dive, leaving me on this world a while longer to spread Their Story.

Prof. Claude: How do you know I was on the beach that morning?

Q: [garbled]

Prof. Claude: Who gave you the permission to read my diary? Who let you in my office? Was it the Dean? That idiot always favored—

Q: [garbled]

Prof. Claude: Okay. Okay. I'm calm, I'm calm.

Q: [garbled]

Prof. Claude: What are you on about? I did not witness—I know what I saw there. Certainly not Milla Perevana and that boy.

Q: [garbled]

Prof. Claude: ...

Q: [garbled]

Prof. Claude: For—for manslaughter? You've got to be joking. You're arresting them for manslaughter? Sabotage—? I never would've thought. *Unbelievable!*

I went back to Lake Oreyd this morning.

Walking along the shore made my heart pound, I felt as if at an unknown place, my eyes drinking in the scene, yet the old lake was washing up on the old beach, impersonal as ever.

Beautiful as ever.

I made my way around the churches to the water.

I gazed across the shimmering surface, dipped my fingers in the cold water, and smiled.

We were shaking hands goodbye, because the lake is gone, with that enigma in its cold depths begging to be studied and solved. Another lake has taken its place, a deep blue tile in this new mosaic of the world where each part is as great as the sum of all, and that one was shaking hands with me, too, its gentle waves lapping at my fingers, saying hello.

"Lake Oreyd" originally appeared in *Metaphorosis*
on Friday, 24 March 2017

About the author

Damien Krsteski writes SF and develops software. Originally frcm Skopje, Macedonia, he now lives and works in Berlin, Germany. Updates about his fiction can be found on his blog or on Twitter.

monochromewish.blogspot.com

A Nightingale's Map of the City

Suzanne J. Willis

The white stone buildings of the city gleam like scattered pearls, their peaks and towers reaching for the vertiginous blue of the sky. Atop the spires and turrets and minarets, domes and curlicues of gold-leaf sparkle, making the city seem dusted with slow-burning embers. The ghost of the giant Gustav, the city's architect and creator, walks cobbled alleyways that are carpeted in moss, skimming past the tiny ferns growing from arched doorways. It is the city he built for his flame-haired Julietta. His place of torment since the day she left.

Everywhere – *everywhere* – are monuments to Julietta. Ivy-covered statues, beaten copper friezes, emerald-roofed cenotaphs carved with elegiac verses. As though all of them together might be woven into a spell under the splinter-moon to bring her back again. Julietta left the city long ago, much longer than Gustav cares to remember. So he holds the city close like a well-worn photograph, folded and re-folded and disintegrating with time. Without it, he's scared that he wouldn't remember her face, her voice, the touch of her skin.

Sometimes, he thinks he sees her as a silver shadow slipping through the streets, leaving an unearthly sheen on the darkening stone. In spring, he glimpses her running in her yellow velvet cape towards the opera house, flanked by the singing fae who bear the remnants of her voice.

Gustav tries to be content with the scraps time has left behind. But doubt frays his edges. Once, this was a city for two. But before she left, Julietta opened the city to mortals, left it behind for them like a discarded toy. He can't remember if, in doing so, she had been deliberately cruel or just thoughtless. The people now living there are tiny and insignificant and shiver just a little when they pass through Gustav's ghost as he sits by the glass butterfly house or, in petulant moments, sprawls across the palace steps.

In the city of giants, of grandeur and vast sorrow, jewels and alabaster, red-haired sylphs float, unseen by its inhabitants, who are busy in the business of being ordinary. They are wisps of women, a thousand images of Julietta woven and rewoven, painted and sung, sculpted and remembered and reshaped in the years since she left.

Red-haired sylphs float as twists of breeze or phrases of song the ear can't quite catch. They drift and glide, wrapped in tresses studded with tiny blue flowers, smiling lasciviously at Gustav, who can only watch as people overrun his city.

He stares at the sky. He wonders, yet again, if one day the sylphs will forget him, too.

They wrap themselves around him and whisper

We are echoes, too.

Gustav shakes them free. He does not feel like listening to them today, whispering in her voice about the roads she might have taken, the places she might be found. Reminding him that he no longer remembers exactly the colour of her eyes, or whether she smelled of rosewater or sandalwood. As though unfolding the old photograph, he traces his hands over the lines of the buildings and the streets, where each day the gold dulls a little, the cobbles wear just a bit more. Only the ghosts of giants and half-maidens who were never more than an imitation remember how it felt when the city had its soul. The warm pliability of compliant stone; the seasons that formed themselves around Julietta's moods.

The door to the palace, banded with iron curled into daemons and lovers and winged serpents that change with the light, resists his touch. Beyond are frescoed rooms, gas lamps and clockwork faeries to serve a princess's every need. But the door stands firm, the treasures beyond it shielded from sight.

The longer she is gone, the more your city slips away from you. Only the doors with gilded handles are open to you now, the sylphs sigh. Gustav can count those handles on one hand. They fade further every day. He sits heavily on the marble outside the butterfly house – to the mortals it feels like a squall of wind gusting by – and presses his ghostly nose to the glass. Butterflies – sapphire, citrine, fuchsia, amber – flit up to him as though he is a honeyed treat laid out by their keepers. Above the entrance, a clockwork butterfly, an imitation of the real ones inside, flutters its wings, takes flight on the quarter hour then lands again. The sylphs stroke Gustav's hands, trying to cheer him in their sweetly savage way.

Once upon a time, an emperor's courtiers built a nightingale from glass and rubies and gold and ribbons. The emperor loved the clockwork bird much more than he had ever loved the real one, with her plain brown feathers and unpredictable tune. Yet she continued to love him long after he had forgotten her in favour of the imitator.

The giant poked his finger moodily at the glass, scattering the butterflies.

Your Julietta, she waited for you as long as she could, dearest, while you were building her memorials. She had cities inside her, waiting for you. Vast and unpredictable and waiting to be explored. One day, all the doors here will be closed to you and you will just be thunder fading in the distance. That is the way of echoes, dear Gustav.

If they weren't so like her, he would wrap their flaming tresses around their throats. Swallows dart and swoop from the sky, skimming through his chest in a gust of air. He follows them as they make their way back to their nests in the city's walls, which were carved with stories written for Julietta, lit at different hours by the sun or moon. The swallows have burrowed through the words so the stories are now just nonsense phrases.

...creature   of   star-flecked   night,   chasing a hollow moon and ever-ebbing tides...

...she reaches for the belly of winter, pushing against diaphanous clouds...

...silver and green, its rhythm mirroring the ocean crashing through her, speaking to the moon moths and wind-ridden gulls...

Is there nothing left in the city that remains as it was in the beginning?

Gustav walks along the wall, reading its broken stories in the late afternoon light. He stops at the southwest corner, where he had long ago tethered a hot air balloon to the wall with creeping vines of purple roses and ruby-seeded pomegranates. He used to bring Julietta here, lift her up to sit in the basket to view the city, its architecture his ever-expanding love letter to her. Surely she had never doubted his heart, laid bare in the streets and passageways and grand buildings with their solid language of stone? But it is this corner to which she made her own way one day, climbing the tethers and scattering purple blooms and red, red seeds in her wake. It is the corner from which she made her escape.

The word jolts Gustav and he repeats it aloud, rolls it around on his tongue. "Escape. Escape..." Until today, he had always thought of her as running away, having left him and spurned his gift of her own city. But that word – *escape* – bubbled up from a forgotten city deep inside him.

Another broken story on the wall glows golden in the afternoon light; like the gilded handles, it admits him to somewhere that could easily have been lost.

...true, you are skin-hungry, your desire washed to a faded wraith-story of missing her. But it was not she who doubted....

With that quiet realisation, Gustav sees his city as Julietta must have seen it, in the end.

"My dearest Julietta, there is nothing of you here," he whispers to the swallows as they dive through air. The rose vine is just thorns now, tangled among the pomegranates that have run wild. As he speaks, one of the wispy wraiths, a distant echo of Julietta whose colour has faded to a rosy silver, snakes through the vine. She beckons to him, giggling, and curls herself at the base of one of the rose bushes.

He pushes his hands through the vines towards her. She fades until nothing is left but a beating light the colour of the sun. Reaching further, towards the buttery glow, Gustav wishes that he could feel the thorns scratching at his skin. Chunks from the wall are scattered among the gnarled roots of the bush, the carved words insensible as even sentences, let alone stories.

Curlew. Spice. Glimmer-deep. Longing.

Two of those clay-cast words glow in the aftermath of the sylph's touch, a lighthouse call across the years to Gustav.

Find me.

They gleam brighter as he stares at them. **Find me.**

He thinks about all the things that she loved: moonlight, early morning, stone bridges over fast-flowing rivers. He smiles as the memories rush through him pulse-quick. Bitter chocolate, wild storms, autumn frost, the light of deepest winter.

He stares at the sky. He wonders. Then he begins to run, along the wall, through the gates, up and down the streets until he finds the sylphs giggling and splashing in the city's central fountain.

What happened to the emperor? Gustav asks.

The clockwork bird ran down and the real nightingale came back, singing him songs from the cherry tree, singing him back from death.

The sun sets, the changeling light serpentine as it twists through hidden alleys and doorways collapsing on themselves. Gustav lies on the cold earth as the sylphs pull the darkness over themselves like a blanket. Sighing, crooning, slipping into sleep.

This city is a story no-one bothers to read, a clockwork nightingale whose gears have rusted silent. But as Gustav lies down next to his red-haired sylphs who smell of cinnamon and autumn, he no longer sees Julietta's pale flesh in the alabaster stone. Julietta's smile peeking from the ivy statues. Julietta's touch in the mist that rolls from the palace windows.

He stares at the indigo sky. He knows what he must do.

Tomorrow, the city may fade a little more, but it no longer matters, for he will not be here to witness it. Tomorrow, he will leave from the corner of roses and pomegranates, and follow the winds that took her away. With those two burning bright words – **find me** – he will search across lands and ocean, seasons and storms.

He will find her and they will build a new city together, one of bridges and clock towers without hands to stop the passage of time. A city not of stone, but of all the thoughts and longings unspoken that fill the spaces between the rooftops and hover above the streets. With sylphs and olive-plump moons and infinite brightness inked by their careful hands. A city that they will call home, with unchartered streets they will explore together. Be she old and faded, or bones and ghost, Julietta will write her own words on the walls and

Gustav will beg her leave to map the cities running wild inside her.

"A Nightingale's Map of the City" originally appeared in *Metaphorosis* on Friday, 10 February 2017

About the author

Suzanne is a Melbourne, Australia-based lawyer and writer. Her spare moments are spent with stories and music. There is a garden outside her little library that was built in the hope that the stories and the greenery might coax the faeries to make a home there. Her tales are inspired by fairytales, ghost stories and all things strange, but her favourite time is spent chilling out at home with her patient partner and pampered pooch.

Suzanne can be found online at suzannejwillis.webs.com

Angels at the Border

Ian Rennie

The angels moved up the road towards Gethsemene in a triad formation. If they'd walked, that would have been something. If they'd flown, swooped in from the sky, that would have been something else. But they didn't. They just moved, floating slowly along the road in unison. Behind them — almost too far away to see — was the unnatural mountain of their home, fading into the skyline.

Valeria had gate duty that day. It was good foraging weather, the kind that would have had Anthony heading out into the wilderness if he were still alive. He had never been able to get Justin interested in the great outdoors, even before the boy was lost to them.

She spotted the three angels as they passed the mile marker and followed them in her riflescope until they reached the gate five minutes later. Twelve miles an hour; slow enough to know they'd be seen.

"That's far enough," Valeria called down as the trio reached the gates. "State your business."

The lead of the group turned to look at her. They weren't identical, just close to it. This one had a broad nose and chubby cheeks that looked out of place on its smooth metallic face.

It spoke in a liquid voice. "We are—"

"I know what you are," Valeria interrupted. "State your business."

The lead angel continued undaunted. "We are a diplomatic delegation and we wish to present credentials. Our common names are—

"Don't care. Do you have business to state or do I have to see you off our property?"

The angel paused. If it had still been a human, Valeria was pretty sure it would have sighed. "Under the terms of the Treaty of Vancouver, diplomatic delegations may approach a freehold when their presence is requested by an inhabitant. Such a request has been made."

Valeria tightened her grip on the rifle. There was only one reason someone would ask for the angels. "You've come for one of us."

"We've come at the request of one of you," the angel replied. "We wish to present credentials."

Valeria sighed. They weren't going to leave any time soon. "Come through to the courtyard. But no further."

She pushed the gate control and stepped down from the watchtower, still holding the rifle. Her left knee was stiff from standing still for too long, and she had to hobble down the tower stairs. By the time she reached the courtyard, the angels were already there, floating unmoving in the centre of the walled space. Close to, they seemed even less human. Their shape was still bipedal and humanoid, but their constituent parts were only loosely attached, as if their thin limbs floated near their torsos rather than being tethered to them.

"So, you taking one of our parents or one of our children?" Valeria asked.

The lead angel looked at her and frowned. "I don't understand your question," it said in its liquid voice.

"Only two types of people summon you," Valeria replied. "Children wanting to rebel or old people wanting another chance. Which is it this time?"

The angel paused again. "The request came from Tamar Antonia Halverston, eighteen years old, of Melchior Plaza, Freehold of Gethsemene. We don't answer requests from children."

"You just did," Valeria grumbled, pulling out a computer pad and tapping instructions into it. After a moment she frowned. "Apparently she's waiting outside. She didn't tell anyone you were coming."

"This is not unusual," the angel said. "We have found that families try to stop the upgrade process."

"I wonder why?" Valeria spat.

The angel looked at her; she could make out the ghosts of pupils in its silver eyes. "As do I," it replied.

The door on the other side of the courtyard opened. As it did, Valeria raised her rifle slightly. If any one of them so much as looked towards the interior of Gethsemene...

They didn't. They floated exactly where they were as the girl entered the courtyard. Hard not to think of her as a girl. Tamar was skinny and undersized, looking closer to twelve than to eighteen. She looked around the courtyard nervously, scratching a spot on the dark skin of her arm. Justin had done the same in his last days, like he thought his skin was the wrong size. Like he wanted to scratch it off and find something else underneath.

"You just stay where you are for now, honey," Valeria said. "You don't have to go anywhere you don't want to."

The lead angel turned smoothly towards the girl. "Tamar Antonia Halverston. We have received a request from you for upgrade. Under the terms of the Treaty of Gethsemene we are here to perform the sublimation process, should you still wish it."

The girl said nothing, just looked at the angels and the woman with the gun, as if uncertain what to do.

Finally Valeria broke the silence. "Tamar, if you want these... *people* to leave, you just need to say the word, all right? If they've got no business here I'll set them on their way."

"I—" Tamar started. Her high voice cracked and caught in her throat.

"Go on, darlin'," Valeria said softly. "Say what you need to say."

"I don't want to live like this anymore," Tamar said. "I want the upgrade."

Valeria let out an angry sigh but tried not to let it show on her face. "I guess that's it, then," she said to the lead angel. "Take your property and get out."

The angel looked at her for a moment. "Standard practice is for the sublimation process to take place here."

Valeria felt bile rise at the prospect. "No way. I can't stop you taking the girl, but I sure as hell can stop you butchering her in front of me."

"There is no butchery. The procedure is—"

"I don't care how clean and hygienic the murder is," Valeria snapped. "It's still murder."

There was a long pause and Valeria knew she had gone too far. This was way past protocol, almost enough to cause a diplomatic incident. Nonetheless she couldn't back down. Not now. Not in front of these bastards.

Salvation came unexpectedly from Tamar. "I want them to do it here," she said, her voice less faltering than it had been before. "I want to leave my old life behind, right here."

The lead angel turned to the girl and nodded, then turned back to Valeria. "We will need a quiet space where we will not be interrupted. The process will take nineteen minutes."

Valeria sighed, her second defeat during this conversation. "There's a room in the guard tower," she said. "A changing room. Kind of appropriate."

"Thank you," the lead angel said. The other two angels floated towards Tamar.

Valeria pinched her fingers on the bridge of her nose. "I can show you the way if—"

"We know the way," the lead angel replied. "We have used the room before."

Tamar walked towards the guard tower, flanked by angels. The lead angel stayed in position in the courtyard.

"Ain't you going with them?" Valeria asked.

The lead angel shook its head. "Only two are necessary for sublimation, and they are more experienced."

"So you're, what, here as back up?"

"You might call me a liaison," the angel said.

"Here to stop me interfering with this 'sublimation' of yours?"

"If you like," the angel replied. "Or here as a hostage in case we do something you don't care for."

Valeria paused. She hadn't thought of it like that. "So if something goes wrong with the girl…"

"Your weapon is powerful enough to kill me, yes. You could kill me now if you were so inclined. I can't speak to what would happen after that."

Valeria realised she was pointing the rifle directly at the angel, and lowered it. "How long did you say this would take?"

"Nineteen minutes," the angel replied. "Seventeen now. If you're worried about Tamar, the process is quite painless."

"So's lethal injection," Valeria snapped.

"Nobody who had a lethal injection could tell you about it afterwards. Having experienced the sublimation process I can guide you through it if you would like. The initial scan of mind-state activity is swift and has already been completed, as has the creation of the primary nanite array. What takes the time is the synchronisation of the array with the existing mind state to create the thoughtform, and the decompliation of—"

"Enough!" Valeria barked. "I don't need to know every detail of what you're doing to her. It's enough to know you bastards won't stop until there are none of us left."

"Logically that's accurate as we will always offer sublimation to those who desire it," the angel replied. "Rhetorically it's not accurate to frame this as a takeover or a conquest. If our desire was simply to sublimate you all we could have done so half a century ago."

"Instead you just let us waste away in goddamn wildlife reserves!"

"The settlements were your idea," the angel answered. "I believe your constitution calls Gethsemene 'A place for humans to be humans'. We would happily make room for you in the arcologies, or build one for you, but both options were rejected by your leadership."

Valeria felt a bitter reply form in her mouth, but swallowed the venom down. "Let's—" she began. "Let's talk about something else. You, maybe. Where are you from?"

"I live in the Bei Hanto Xa arcology. Outside of my liaison duties, I spend my time—"

"I don't care about the arcologies. You said you'd been through the upgrade. You were a human once. Where are you from?"

The angel paused. "It's considered impolite to talk about our origins," it said. "It separates those whose thoughtform originates in a human mind from those produced through algorithmic blending."

Valeria looked away. The last thing she wanted to hear about was the sex lives of these damn things.

"However, you weren't to know that," the angel continued. "Yes, my thoughtform was human once. Before my sublimation I lived in the Britannia settlement."

Valeria snorted disbelief. "Britannia fell apart a century ago. The survivors came here. My grandma told me about it."

"Yes," the angel replied.

"Are you trying to tell me you've been alive for–"

"It's considered impolite to talk about our origins," the angel repeated.

Valeria sighed, and unclipped a pouch on her belt. "Do you eat or drink?" she asked.

"I can," the angel replied. "We don't have to, but many of us choose to."

Valeria pulled two sticks of soy jerky from the pouch and handed one to the angel. She tensed as its hand came near to hers, but concentrated on her breathing until the angel withdrew with the stick.

She leaned against a wall and chewed her jerky, not taking her right hand off the rifle. She flexed her left leg, trying to work off the dull ache in the knee. After she was finished with the jerky, she stared at the angel for a moment, deep in thought.

"I went to school with kids from Britannia families," Valeria said eventually. "Each of them had family stories about the fall and the exodus. I knew a boy whose great grandfather died on the trip over. Why didn't you help them?"

"We did," the angel said. "We gave you as much help as you were willing to take. By the time it was disbanded there were less than a thousand people in Britannia: barely enough to keep the machinery of the settlement together, not enough to support it for any longer."

"How *could* there be?" Valeria asked, angrily. "You take their kids. You take their grandparents. You leave nothing behind."

"We take only those who wish to go. We give the rest of you the best life we can."

Valeria stood up straight, feeling the stiffness and pain in her back and her leg. "I had a son once," she said, not sure why she was telling the angel this. "Justin was a beautiful boy, smartest kid you ever met. He played the violin like an angel. Better than an angel, like a *human*. I loved him as much as he loved me, as much as he hated this place, this 'best life' you've given us. The day he turned eighteen he called out to you and you took him away from me."

The angel floated, unmoving and silent. "I'm sorry for your pain," it said eventually. "You must have loved him very much."

"As much as his father did. Anthony couldn't take the loss of his son, couldn't live in this world without his boy. He stole my sidearm and walked out into the wilderness where I wouldn't have to deal with his body. I guess he thought he was being kind. He took himself away, but I still blame you. Can you see why your 'best life' is a bunch of shit?"

She turned and walked away from the angel. As she did, her knee started to buckle. She steadied herself on the wall.

"Are you all right?" the angel asked.

"Old injury that still plays up," Valeria said. "It's worse in winter."

She felt the angel's hand on her shoulder, soft and cold.

"We could help you with that," the angel said in its soft, liquid, inhuman voice.

Valeria spun round, rifle raised. "I swear to fucking God, if you ever touch me again I'll kill every one of you bastards!"

Despite the angel's impassive face, it seemed suddenly angry. "I was trying to help!" it snarled, its voice louder and more forceful than she had heard it before. "All we have ever wanted to do is to help you!"

"And all we've wanted you to do is to leave us the fuck alone!" Valeria snapped.

"Do you have any idea what it would mean if we left you alone?" the angel asked. "We give you clement weather, clean energy, machines that never break. If we left you alone you'd all be dead within the decade."

"Well, maybe we'd prefer that to being pets!"

Before anything else could be said, the door to the guard tower opened and the three angels emerged. They were near identical. Valeria spent a moment scanning their faces to see if she could tell which had been Tamar.

It didn't matter. Tamar was dead. This was just what they had done with her remains.

"Our business here is completed," the lead angel said.

"Good," Valeria replied. "Get the fuck off our property."

Valeria didn't watch them leave. The angels returned to the heaven they had built, and she walked back into Gethsemene. She was rostered as sentry for another two hours, but right now she didn't want to look at the world, at anything.

She thought about going to Melchior Plaza. Someone would have to tell Mr and Mrs Halverston what had happened to their little girl; someone would have to destroy their lives just as someone had destroyed Valeria's.

Instead she went home, to the two-bedroom apartment that was too big for her, crowded with memories of the past. She went into Justin's old room and looked around at the things he had left behind. She picked up his dusty violin, lay on his bed, and waited in vain for the tears to come.

"Angels at the Border" originally appeared in *Metaphorosis*
on Friday, 14 April 2017

About the author

Ian Rennie is a librarian and writer in Cambridge, England. As well as writing, he is one of the Cambridge organizers of National Novel Writing Month. He was once retweeted by Neil Gaiman, not that he's bragging or anything.

ianrennie.wordpress.com

Sharpington Coffers – Current Score: 49.8

Erik Goldsmith

A perfunctory stare hovers above the counter of Sharpington Coffers, a small antique store on the south side of Picadilly Circus. The owner of the stare, one Mr. Bartholomew Sharpington, watches his entrance with the patience of the rat catcher, waiting outside a hole for his prey, his customer, who will be walking through those doors… any… second… now. *Ching. Ching.*

A tall man in a black hat steps into the store and shakes his wet jacket onto the floor without so much as an apology. Sharpington, used to the rudeness of Londoners, pulls his cheeks up into a smile as if…

I can't seem to finish the analogy here. He smiles as if… what?

Some Notes for Future Revision:
- Get rid of the words "perfunctory," "of the store," and "rat catcher" (instead say, "… with the patience of a cat." Or "a cat's patience." Pick one.)
- Get rid of "without so much as an apology." Unnecessary.
- Do you need the *Ching Ching?*
- Don't forget, the Insta-Karma people said that when you remove his visor, make sure the red light is off, even if his identity doesn't take, otherwise

the   degeneration   might   accelerate.   DON'T
FORGET.

A stare hovers above the counter of Sharpington Coffers, a small
antique store on the south side of Picadilly Circus. The owner, one Mr.
Bartholomew Sharpington, watches his entrance with the patience of a
cat waiting outside a hole for its prey, for his customer, who will be
walking through those doors... any... second... now.
A tall man in a black hat steps into the store and shakes his wet jacket
onto the wooden floor. Sharpington, used to the rudeness of
Londoners, pulls up his cheeks into a smile as if editing this story might
take your mind off it... Why are you still trying to fix it anyway? It's just
that... *Sharpington Coffers* isn't going to be published... The 30 polite,
but canned rejection letters seemed to be saying as much... not quite
what they're looking for, they said... *Not quite*, as if my story just
slipped their version of acceptable by a thin margin, as if a human
being had actually read it, as if they hadn't just noticed it's 49.8, and
chunked it in the fucking garbage... I spent an hour on that last
sentence... Flawless.

I don't know if you know this, but the qualifying
score to be considered a creative person is a fucking
50.00; if your story scans below that, well... We all keep
the Creativity Aggregator a secret from the public, but
every publication uses the machine to scan the new
writers... It works better than an intern, but something
is definitely lost without the human touch... At the
office, we set the bar at 50, but I had hoped, I guess... I
had just hoped, for my own sake, that a CA score of 50
wasn't the industry standard... It's hard not to take the
score personally. Some writers can score above a 60
consistently... even without having editorial access to a
CA... But I do have access, and it took four different re-
writes and a bunch of antiquated words just to get
Sharpington Coffers up from a 49.7... And honestly, I

don't even know if it's better for the effort, over-edited doesn't seem like the right word... I've stranged it... combed out every redundancy, every derivation... every similarity to anything in the Library of Congress's database, syntax, flights of language, algorithms of style and word frequency... I know how the machine works, I just can't seem to game it...

When he was still him, Dad told me that the creativity aggregator might make people forget the value of simplicity... I think he meant it as encouragement, but I took it poorly... My story's not simple, I said. None of my stories are simple, I said. But he merely shrugged and told me it wasn't a bad thing... I didn't get what he was saying until it was too late for me to say so... At the time, I just couldn't bring myself to... turn my head towards the right way of looking at it or... I don't know, it's hard to say, and maybe that's my fucking problem. Maybe, you're just not good at this shit... or at least not good enough to write a 9,486 word murder mystery set in Victorian fucking London... The cannibal twist isn't interesting, Sharpington's character is dead on arrival, and no one even remembers what a bicycle is, let alone a torture device made out of one... I can't even remember the story's original score.

A good writer should be able to sense when the creative winds are strong enough to spin the blades of the mill and when they are nothing but a capricious breeze trembling the sails. A good writer would know the difference and a better writer would know when to quit. They'd be able to sense their own lack of subtlety; their inability to penetrate a psychology other than their own... Can a good writer ignore the distortion of self-appreciation? A great writer would be able to feel their entire mechanism faltering under the strain of the task, and just... A non sequitur: Why is it so hard to get published? It seems an odd question to intrude among pretentious speculation, like it jumped the queue, or was the pretentious speculation merely a disguise to hide insecurity... I can fucking hear him... through the wall, I can hear him moaning something about wolves... it sounds so fucking awful, he can't sleep... the visor must be hurting him...

Hector told me he got one for his mom... He said her dementia was gone in the first 6 hours. Now, he says, she walks around the house griping at him about laundry and his ex-wife, which are both totally legitimate concerns as far as Hector goes... He says it's given him a fresh take on annoyance... But, he was lucky... The Insta-Karma people told us we'd know if the visor works within the first 48 hours... It's been 36. After the first 48, the window closes... some identities, they said, for *whatever reason,* can't be re-read once they've slipped away... I'm gonna try to sleep.

I can't sleep... **11 hours**.

I've been staring at the words above my cursor for a while now, and I think I like them better than the 9,500 below it... That's not a good sign... I've been trying to think of something more to say, rubbing my forehead... I don't know why I might need to find some coherence in all this... Fuck, isn't that what that group counselor told you, that you need to externalize... I can't even finish the sentence...

"You're a writer, why don't you try writing it down?" she said. Make something coherent out of what's going on with your life. It'll give you a context for all this, and maybe it'll provide you with a sense of control... She didn't say that last part actually, I just wish she had, but she didn't, because it's probably not true... I need some coffee... I'm going to get coffee...

I'm back... Let's pretend me needing coffee and rubbing my head's enough context for all this... sitting here, drinking coffee... talking to myself... listening to him moan about wolves... pretending this is all a fucking story... Wolves... Is he remembering?

He showed it to me a long time ago, one of the few stories he let me see... What was it? ... A man playing in the snow at night and a wolf. The man was making snow angels with his son, looking up at the stars, and then suddenly a white wolf is standing over both of them. The man rolls on top of the boy, crushing him into the snow, and starts yelling at the wolf to go away. The boy is crying underneath him and tries to push him off, but the dad is too heavy... Stop Moving... I remember Dad stretched the scene out way too long, and made it seem like the boy was suffocating, but he kept using words like "almost" and "just about" for pages. And then with a single sentence the wolf leaves and that's it. "Suddenly, the white wolf padded away and didn't look back." No fireworks, no climax, the wolf just runs away. Or something like that, it's here somewhere... Then they just walk home and the man apologizes to the son and then it ends... I told him it read like a pastoral tone poem, hiding my derision with college. He told me I didn't get it... It's on this computer somewhere.

They scanned it and every other hard drive we had in the house, all our photos, his buying habits, where we've lived, all his unpublished stories, all of it, right before strapping him into a brain scanner... fuck they made me talk to him about mom, while he writhed around, confused... 4 MRI's... We even had to sit across from that young asshole in VR goggles, pantomiming around my father's entire life from the inside, just in case he had a question for us... Did we really need to be there for that?... I suppose digital information can only contain so much information... Is that funny?

By the end of it, the technician printed out an approximate neural map of what my Dad's brain looked like before it deteriorated. I remember staring at it, offended by its visibility. When I asked my Dad if he still wanted to go through with it, to try and remember, he said he did. They fitted him for the Identity Keeper visor, downloaded the map into it, took all my money, and sent us home with a box full of foam packaging.

Some of it spilled on our rug when I pulled the visor out... I remember he took it from my hands, set it in his lap, and intentionally, I know he did, refused to acknowledge it. I remember him turning his head... toward nothing, an open doorway maybe, and interlocking his fingers across his stomach, a familiar posture in the house. Maybe, he remembered sitting with the technician; I wasn't sure, but I let him hold for a few moments. Then I took it back... and put it on his head, and the man. fucking. winced... I saw it. He winced. I couldn't believe it... He didn't tell that fucking technician the visor was hurting him, he told him it felt fine. "Really?" the boy asked. "Usually we have to adjust it..." He let us go home with it after almost no alterations. It's probably still hurting him. I tried to adjust it myself and he made this fucking noise... I've been listening to it all day, this noise, letting it feed me a steady drip of stress at the office... Obviously it wasn't just physical discomfort, because he was smiling too when he made it, but... Imagine you understand the perversity of this situation without knowing the context, or our relationship, which I don't have the skill to adequately express. He moaned because he thought I'd find it funny and he was in pain and he couldn't remember what was going on, but he remembered just enough to be stressed the fuck out. All of it... What time is it? He's got 10 hours... I'll have to call in to work soon, tell them I'm not coming in... They won't need me tomorrow anyway... The whole thing's formatted already. After our editor's meeting, I spent most of today locked in the VR server, updating our author's databases, sending out teaser blurbs about the 8 stories, going over the check list, watching to see if that girl got any branches... **10 hours**...

We got lucky this month. Three giant authors, all-frequencies no less, reached out to our publication in the same week and we snatched them up without reading them. Tremendously well written stories by today's top authors:

1. Johnny Grab - The You in the Light Switch – 4,300 words. - *"A subtle elegy on the various ways one might see death differently... not positively, differently."* (64.8)
2. Obri Okafor - Images of Neo-Glasnost – 8,000 words. - *"Gorgeously worded barbs of deceit and intrigue wrapped around a post-modern essay on contemporary politics."* (59.9)
3. Mia Paladucci - A Tremor Nearer – 2,400 words. - *"Too often short fiction allows us a reprieve from our present day problems without easing us back into the real world, but Paladucci's prose provides us both an escape and return passage back to our own lives, better for the trip."* (60.3)

"The first two are fine, but the Paladucci blurb needs to be re-written. I'm surprised you didn't catch it, Frank." The head editor says this to me in front of the other editors.

"What's wrong with it?" I ask.

"It's just generic, son." he says. "Not incisive." he says. "Keep the alliteration." he says. "Lose the shittiness." he says.

I immediately start re-writing it while he discusses a formatting issue with the Johnny Grab story. I realize my editor sounds like a shitty character; would be a shitty character if it were fiction, and I wonder if it's because I don't understand him; wouldn't bother trying, though. Maybe I'm a good writer after all.

   3. Mia Paladucci - A Tremor Nearer – 2,400 words.
   "Too often short fiction leaves the reader feeling short changed, but Paladucci's prose packs the same punch as a trilogy of novels... simply incredible."

"Better." He admits. "Okay, we've got 5 slots left... and 9 options. I'm assuming we've all read the picks."

There were almost 400 submissions, maybe 500, I could look up the exact number, but a small town sent us their stories ... unimaginable time and effort... And from those, the creativity aggregator decided just 9 were creative enough. It's a big time saver, designed to weed out stories that we shouldn't bother reading. Needless to say, the device cannot truly measure the worth of a good story, but I'd say a good 90% of the time, it's an accurate measure of shit... I usually read one or two of the stories that score below a 50. I've only found 3 that weren't absolute garbage... I don't know what that says about me.

Anyway.

After ditching *them,* the remaining choice is between five stories from semi-established authors with more than 100 pre-downloads and four back-ups with 0 – in other words, newbies. The newbies don't have much of a chance, since our readers customize their subscriptions. Some authors have 100 pre-downloads, some have more than 10,000 (the all frequencies), others have none. The honest truth is that most authors, as in most people, have no pre-downloads, so people, like readers and editors, overlook them. 5 stories. 5 slots. The End. The decision is a foregone conclusion, but it's our dramatic policy to vote on every story, and it's a good thing we do.

We unanimously vote for four of the five established authors without discussion, but the fifth draws debate. It is a woman with just 124 pre-downloads, hundreds less than the other 4 authors. I vote against it like the other editors do, and listen to their complaints. They found it boring. It lacked action, no real hook. They say its themes were heavy handed and the characters didn't seem realistic. One of them says, "Caricatures of archetypes... Lifeless. What is her problem?" I know what her problem is; she's in free-fall. The woman has only been published twice in 6 years, but the memory of being accepted, that sweet dopamine rush, addicted her to this gambling. She couldn't stop trying to get published, even when she began to realize those two stories were flukes. She can't stop. She's not good enough. The hurt claws from her story like a zombie, implying pain between her clumsy syntax and the many skipped words that might as well have been intentional. I say nothing and we dump it like an unread suicide note... **9 hours**.

Which leaves the newbies.

"Any of the other 4 even slightly published?" Asks our lead editor, flipping through the pages. Hector's in charge of our newbie slush pile. He shakes his head.

We look at their titles and the names of the authors. None of us have heard of any of them:

1. "The Trapeze Parallax Quandary." - Temple Ritter
2. "Shotgun Party" - Polita Valdez
3. "A Chance to Remember" - Athena Moonglow
4. "There Won't Be Much Left" - Gretchen Pull

I have no illusions about this process. The reality is that we are deciding which invisible stranger will be dancing around their kitchen in their underwear re-evaluating their own self-worth and which invisible strangers will simply sigh and remind themselves they knew it'd never happen anyway.

"Well, which story should we pick?"

None of my father's stories were ever published. Sometimes, he'd try to hint that I should publish them at my prestigious job, but I didn't bother. My reputation was tenuous as it was, considering that of the 6 editors, I am the only writer without pre-downloads of my own, so I couldn't get published there either... In fact, very few times have I been published at all. Only once at a semi-professional publication early on, a now-defunct paper magazine. It was about a cat that gets run over on a highway. It was a stupid story... When I ran it later, the creativity aggregator only gave it a 52.4, but it was mine and it was published, which is more than I can say of any of my dad's stories... **8 hours**.

"It hurts my ears."

When I tried adjusting it for him, he asked, "What is this thing, Frankie?"

"It's the Insta-Karma Identity Keeper. You wanted it, remember?"

He shrugged as if none of it mattered and looked away, cool and disaffected beneath my hands.

I remember I finished messing with it and asked, "That still hurt?" but he said nothing and interlocked his fingers.

"Hey Pops." I asked. "You said it hurt your ears... does it still hurt?"

"My ears don't hurt." He told me innocently.

Then he told me "all that" foam packaging would need to get cleaned up before I went home. I couldn't believe he said it. It wasn't the nerve of him telling me what to do, but that he thought I was leaving, that I could leave... What did he think home was? How far back did he have to go to believe I was only there for a visit? He pointed to the mess on the floor and smiled like that was the joke. To be honest, this was all his idea, he just can't remember, and this cowardly smile must be so fucking deep within him if he's still doing it by rote. The little disguise of kindness he makes when he imposes on others... My mother once told me that his kindness was never a disguise, after I delivered that line to her in the kitchen. "It's irritating how he disguises imposition with kindness." I said proudly, publishing myself in the air between us, but she overlooked the sentence's deft syntax and literary merit and just told me I didn't know shit about my father. I already knew that.

"I'll clean it up." I said.

"You made a mess."

"I know I did, Pops. s'okay."

He smiled. "It's not that big."

He winked when he said it, and I just seem to... I don't know what I was going to say there. I read over what I wrote, and I'm afraid he's coming off like a sad bastard, and I know that's a cardinal rule for writers: show, not tell, but he's not a sad bastard. He's amazing, and in person his patience still gets translated through him despite his failing mind, but somehow I can't even show it with a few fucking words... I'd have to use flashbacks from other times, of... other things in our lives that penetrated memory, experiences that might show the other side of the coin for you, make it shine underwater. My writer's impulse, another limp breeze, would like to show another flashback, a tender moment between my father and my mother, but I don't want to. I can't think of one... **7 hours**.

A good writer could... and a better writer would have realized there's no more story to tell long before and gone to sleep... They would've quit mid-way through the second paragraph and decided to move on to something else, something easier, something within their framework of experience without simply wallowing in the distortion of self-appreciation or pity, whatever that means... a better writer would make the shit with my father and my stupid job interweave, use them to make sense of the other. Do they offer contextual counterpoint? Do they amplify each other like a goddamn helix because nothing's fucking happening... When Dad finally put it on his head, the red light blinked, and so did Dad. Nothing, but something was supposed to be fucking happening, so, I looked at the instructions again, very aware of his agitation and stress. I had to yell at him not to take it off. He didn't know why he couldn't take it off. I wish he'd forget about anxiety altogether, but that never seems to leave. He's not that far gone... but it's encroaching on us, I can tell. Some secret whisper, some inside joke he's hearing out of context... In fact, Jesus, that's what it's all about, isn't it? The slow slip from context. Fragments. Dropping dishes. Staring at something uninteresting too long. I don't know. The way he starts doing some things and not doing others. Improvising... Trying to clean the food off his plate, scraping it into the sink even though he's still hungry...

It's supposed to have been cured by now. They've been telling him this his whole fucking life... Advancement after god damn advancement, just a few more years and they'd have it. The future will save you... "With VR imagery we can analyze the micro-biology of neural pathways to best determine how to restrict degeneration and possibly... " He's getting up. He's using the bathroom... At least, we're not there yet... He's got **6 hours** left and she still hasn't gotten any branches... Since, I run the publication's servers, I can monitor the database from home, but there's only so much I can do with my Dad's desktop... I had planned on buying a VR hook up so I could actually work on the server from home, but instead I bought an expensive hat... I might be able to get a cheaper one later this year, but it won't be one with the same visualization...

Interweave.

Imagine a giant globe; not outside of one, but rather inside... you're inside this giant 1,000 foot VR globe. It's filled with blinking lights all around. Thousands and thousands of different colored lights fold across your horizon. Every light is one of our subscribers, and the light's variegated color is actually code for that particular subscriber's location, among other things, like credit card information blah blah blah. But you're inside of it and it is massive. You'll have to look up because the interface doesn't let you fly around or anything, just kind of situates you at the base of the sphere in front a 1,000 foot translucent column of light that stretches all the way to the top of the globe. This simple visual is actually the... you know, just imagine I said some inscrutable techno-nonsense like most sci-fi writers do and pretend I know what I'm talking about... The file, some story we're publishing, waits beside me like a giant firefly winking soft purple and gray plush and when I pull it into the beam, it floats up the column of light towards the very center of globe. It is very beautiful, because... it's just beautiful, and as it ascends, the story stops in the globe's center, gently hovering in the air. Then, it explodes. Branches of white light burst from the author's story towards pre-downloaded subscribers, growing into a giant tree of pure light. Each branch a memory. In real life, the story is simply being uploaded into the public access servers, but in the VR space, it appears like it is being raptured up to heaven, not a joke... barely figurative. Potentially thousands of people might access it, converting it to memory, immortalizing it. It's as good a rapture as any.

I sit inside the VR globe sometimes, pretending to work, and watch the process as a little known author's story finds its readers. Unlike the automatic pre-downloads, the voluntary downloads grow, not from the story outward, but from the reader, reaching inward, like a hand. I always see it like that, like a hand, from the reader to the story. The dim beam emerges from the subscriber, a single point of color and slowly extends into the center beam, so that column and branch become one. Then they read it. Every sentence that passes through a reader's processors, makes the branch become brighter and brighter and brighter... Some readers quit midway, and after a week the beam spreads the accumulated glitter across its length, gradating the dim inwards... saving memory. Let's say I described that well enough... But, if the reader finishes the story, the beam turns into a solid white light, fully downloaded into the reader's memory banks. Once this happens, famous author or not, there is no way to tell which branches were pre-downloaded and which were voluntary. They all look alike. By the end of the month, most of our stories look like luminous pixelated trees, a shimmering digital core floating within it like a sleeping princess waiting to be kissed. Then, we flush it, waive our rights, and start again... **5 hours**.

Uploading an all-frequency is not as beautiful as uploading a story with only 500 pre-downloads, because there's no nuance to the form, no subtlety, no anticipation... just an immediate transference. They do not look like trees with branches in various states of glow, they look like fucking sunbursts. These people are so famous, that every one of our readers has digitally said, "I want any story by this author downloaded directly into my brain. No questions asked." Sometimes, I wonder if the other editors even bother reading them. I wouldn't blame them if they didn't. What would be the point? They float up and then, boom, sun. And, maybe this is the jealousy talking, but I'd bet that stories who get their branches from subscriber to story voluntarily are often better... Truth be told, I've found a few stories by all-frequencies that scored below a 50. We don't run all-frequencies through the aggregator, but I do, just to see... just like I sneak in and run my own stories... Flawless segue.

"What are the newbies' scores?"

"77.8, 58.2, 57.1, and 60.6."

"Is the 77.8 the parallax one?"

Hector nods.

"Did it gets its score for the reasons I think it did?"

He nods again.

"Well then, don't include it next time... The 60, which one's that?"

"It's called "A Chance to Remember" by Athena Moonglow?" The newbie editor's voice rises like it's a question, "It's good."

"Shitty title... Shitty fake name... Fine. We'll load it up. Does it need any work?"

"Some, but—"

"Anybody else read it?" he asks.

I did. She speaks with the voice of someone who has known real loss, her words shaped around the outlines of... absences, ghosts, things that weren't there, presences, and not just implications. She's got it... but I take too long to say so.

"No one? Well, let's upload it anyway. We're already set this month." He shrugs at the newbie editor. "Hopefully someone'll read it besides you."

Not an idle threat... I've seen a few stories go the full month without getting a single branch. They just hang there in our server for 30 days like a ghostly tree trunk, uncommitted to memory. Athena Moonglow...

I am in the doorway when Hector tells Athena Moonglow her story has been accepted. She screams so loud the display glitches and he has to call her back. She claps and agrees to everything he asks. We're addicting her to gambling, just like the woman with 124 pre-downloads. I have to leave the room. For some reason, we treat her like a professional writer and give her online access to her own download stats, so she can sit there and watch how many people read her story... or don't read her story... all month. I'm worried for her... My father was so cavalier about his own rejections. It wasn't that the editors didn't get it, he'd say, it was that they couldn't... He's moving around again, I can hear the mattress creaking... Maybe it's hurting his ears again, maybe it got roughed by the pillow when he came from the bathroom. I tried tilting it before he went to bed so that the diodes weren't rubbing against his temple, but then he started telling me a story about something he and mom did a few years ago... Then, he looked around and asked me about her... wondered where she was. I started to make something up, then I just said I didn't know, which was the truth, and let him go... **4 hours**.

Let's say I manage to tie these two narratives together into a satisfying conclusion. If I were a better writer though, I'd just stop now, instead of sitting here at 5 AM waiting for my dad to wake up and watching the stats for *A Chance to Remember*. It's a stupid fucking title. It's been in the public server all day and nothing. Not a single download... Athena Moonglow... A non sequitur: Why would anyone label themselves that on purpose? The name shrieks insecurity. It begs the game of Jungian shadows, right? We have to assume that Ms. Matthews, or whatever her real name is, I didn't check, would be sifting through her own potential memories, an avid reader herself, and a new name would pop across her perception, why, it's an author she's never heard of before. Athena Moonglow... 'What a name!?!' She'd think. 'This fellow goddess cloaks herself in the diction of mystery and power; therefore, her narratives must be weighted with the grace evoked from a supreme feminine majesty... just. like. me!' And then, Ms. Matthews would instantly download the new author's story simply because of the name, Athena Moonglow... The name surely echoes when you say it out loud. This young girl, watching her screen, refreshing the page again and again... The worst part was the sight of her stupid novelty glasses bobbing around her excited face; the frames were MOON SHAPED! Imagine that. Whoever she meets, she knows the moment her fancy pseudonym drops, the mystery will begin to unravel. They'll make the connection... 'Their eyes seem to be focused on *something*,' she'd think to herself... but she knows where they're looking; what they're thinking. They are assigning her, Ms. Matthews, depth; a depth that is not suggested by her common name and her common face. Name. Glasses. Name. Glasses. She wouldn't dare draw attention to it, but she'll let them figure it out for themselves like a good author. And because she's afraid she isn't what she wants to be, she uses her glasses, just like her name, as a not-so-subtle instruction for others to know how they should see her, how colorful she is, how quirky. It's a verifiable fact, look at my fucking glasses. 'Here's a girl that has the creative spark bubbling beneath those unique rims.' She'd think they think... and we must assume that Ms. Matthews believes the rest of the world operates using that exact same inanity, opening their mouths, stretching out their sanitized tongues, waiting for the right words to trigger their

It's six in the morning. I'm holding the visor. He walked in and made me take it off him. He's back in bed now... I've put it on my own head. Don't worry, I made sure the red light was off. That'd be strange, wouldn't it? De-limited to only think and feel like my dad... used to. I could access his memories... but only the way he used to perceive them. Strange. I'm not even sure it works like that, but it sounds like an interesting story... Best to leave it for a better writer. I'm too good for it.

The thing finally uploaded his identity at 6:12 in the A.M. **Almost 45 hours later**. It worked. He woke up, himself again, and the first thing he remembered was her. My Dad, fully my Dad, made me take it off him. I tried to make my Dad keep it on, talk to my Dad, reason with my Dad, but he didn't want it and he handed it back to me, cognizant of what it meant. I couldn't help but tell him I love him, and watch him, sentient, process the words before he faded from me again... smiling all the way down. He knew it was an imposition on me.

His tree, the map of his identity... they gave me a copy of it. Oh my God, that, *A Chance to Remember,* I swear I'm not doing it on purpose like those fucking glasses... Anyway, I had the thought, at the time, that the file's programming appeared as text, or could be translated into it at least. I said so to the technician and he told me "sure." It's not farfetched. The text appears linear, from top to bottom, or rather inside-out. From core motivations outward to convictions, beliefs, contradictions toward quirk, minutiae, preference. Beginning, Middle, and End. Trunk, branch, leaf. Parts 1, 2, and 3. Each particular is punctuated with a quantized memory, the one most idiosyncratically aligned with the neural shape to serve as an example of the programming's... what... veracity? A flashback, I guess. The whole thing comes to around 6,500 words, a short story. Of course, it occurred to me to upload it.

I'd watch my father's identity, rise into the air, and witness reader after reader reach out to his story and dedicate it to their memory. The branches of light, a multiplicity, plenary apotheosis, a sycamore of pure energy goading forever to chuckle at the seed of his former limitation, until it finally became the sun itself... Or... all the more likely, no one would read it and it'll just sit there in the upload beam for a month ghosting, and then I'd get fired. It probably wouldn't get above a 50 on the aggregator anyway. That's not to say it's bad, just not original... But, I wouldn't fucking know. I'm not reading it.

Athena still has no downloads. I want to anonymously tell her that when we publish even one all-frequency, let alone three, chances are, people will venture out less. Usually, people only read one story a month. Space is a commodity... It doesn't mean her story is bad. It's just that everything unfamiliar is an unread magazine beside a mental toilet. Choice is hard. If a subscriber didn't pre-download it, they'd have to manually click on it and brave the potential for boredom without spraying pre-nostalgia all over their experience like pesticide. They'd have to decide to read something new without any memories, commercials of familiarity, providing a cozy context for the story's consumption... I'm not going to do it.

I thought about buying a subscription under my dad's name and pre-downloading Athena Moonglow, subscribing to her. She'd see it, know someone read her story, but so would the other editors. They know my name, my Dad's name, Sr. I'm not going to do it.

You know, when I first started editing *Sharpington Coffers* two years ago, I was so egotistical as to imagine that each tiny change was so profound, would be so appreciated, that I actually... I actually imagined releasing it as a book, from first draft to final draft, each re-iteration a chapter... I wonder if good writers aggrandize their own thoughts into narration, the way shitty writers do... Maybe good writers know the difference between what is story and what is simply themselves.

The visor is heavier than it looks and it's hurting my ears... I take it off and set it on some of Dad's legal junk. He's not going to wear it. I should've known. He'll never wear it... and it was so damn expensive, too. The thought makes me laugh... I'm going to bed.

Some Notes for Future Revision:
- Write an epilogue. Explain how you randomly found this file a week ago, and when you ran it through the creativity aggregator without the vestigial 9,500... IT GOT A 54.7! Talk about how you're thinking about publishing it, as is...
- Try to fix it so you don't come across like an asshole...
- Delete extraneous ellipses and the sentence fragments.
- Re-write VR process imagery without the self-conscious nonsense.
- Tie up Athena Moonglow thing. Find out how many reads she got last month, like 100 or something. Talk about how that's not bad for a new writer. (Change her name and that embarrassing title... maybe, pretend the whole thing is fiction... like you wrote it all on purpose.)
- Mention how the woman with 124 pre-downloads still hasn't published anything... Why would you do that?
- Re-iterate how you know you'll have to re-write the whole thing - Tie into the ending somehow. Should you bookend the thing by finishing the paragraph you started at the beginning?
- Pick a tense.
- Pick a point of view.
- Re-write descriptions of Dad's personality. They're not right and sound incomplete. Include a

flashback with Mom, and write a better summary for his wolf story. You could do better.

- In epilogue of story, include how you've tried putting the visor on him again, but each time, 45 hours later, he makes you take it off. Talk about how you knew he would, but you do it anyway just to see him in that moment. I've done it 8 times... Don't include that. Maybe write some poetic nonsense... a happy ending?
- *"My dad was the perfect reader for his own story, but in the end, even he didn't want to read it. It didn't let him escape, but instead brought him back to reality... 4 out 5 stars."* (Revise.)
- Since it's fiction now, what is the overall task the narrator cannot seem to accomplish? His writing, some anger he can't express... Does the narrator worry whether his father knows he loves him? Can he adequately express it? (Revise thematic questions.)
- And since it's fiction now, tie the happy ending into the speculation about writing from the beginning... Is there a sense of authorship that accompanies a memory, something that brings it to life? Is that good? Tie this question of the authorship of memories throughout, and for the final paragraph, write a gentle meditation about revision, hinting at the parallel with real life... don't make it obvious.
- And since it's fiction, make it seem like the narrator got a higher score on the aggregator... 64.9 or higher... and change the title to "Wolves." It'll sound cooler.

"Sharpington's Coffers - Current Score 49.8" originally appeared in Metaphorosis on Friday, 8 December 2017

About the author

Erik Goldsmith is a high school English teacher in Houston. He lives with his wife and son.

Sundown on the Hill

Timothy Mudie

Judy wakes up in the middle of the night to an empty bed, but she knows exactly where Edward is. There's only one place he goes these days. As she lies there in the late summer heat, the sheet sticky on her legs, a fan blowing desultorily from an open window, she allows herself a moment to believe he might simply be making one of his many nightly trips to the bathroom. That he has gone to the kitchen for a glass of water. That she will pad from the bedroom down the hall and find him watching an old Western TV program with the volume turned down low and the closed captioning on. But the moment passes, and she climbs from bed, confirms that Edward is missing, slips on a pair of laceless sneakers, and retrieves her keys from the rack by the front door.

She pauses there, looking down at herself. Pajamas and sneakers. She could go back to bed. Edward is a grown man, her husband, someone who should be able to take care of himself. What is the worst that would happen if she left him to go on these jaunts alone? Some early morning jogger or birder stumbling across him and bringing him home just after sunrise. Judy opening the door to find Edward on the front step, embarrassed and shoeless. But she can't do that, can't turn him into some lost puppy. The thought flits from her mind quicker than a firefly's burst of light. Edward is her husband, and he is still here. She will help him as she can.

Outside, Judy is greeted by the chorus of crickets and other night insects. A whippoorwill chortles its familiar call in the distance. She adds her Chrysler's purring engine to the nighttime song.

The roads are clear as she drives out of the town proper and into the park, streetlights becoming sparser along the way. Though she has spent her life in this part of upstate New York, it always awes her how dark and still it is this late at night. Edward had moved here for just that reason, to be close to Sharp Hills State Park. She realizes that she has never seen this park in daylight, and doubts Edward has either. He decided to live here to be near the park, and what he wants in the park only exists in the night.

The park is closed to the public at this time, the lot empty as Judy pulls in, the moon the only light. She knows the paths well enough by now to walk them by memory. Edward expects to see more than moonlight up above, longs for it. Judy doesn't, but looks anyway. Confirms that the only light in the sky is natural.

She comes upon Edward in his usual spot, standing on the nearest hilltop, in the center of a small clearing. Hunched, his knees bent, but always standing. Tonight he wears a pair of khakis with a striped button-down and tie. Like he's heading to work, though they've both been retired for the past five years.

Looking upward, always looking upward, Edward doesn't notice Judy until she puts her hand on his shoulder. He starts, then gives her a sad smile.

"I thought tonight would be the night," he says. "No such luck, I guess."

The sun will be up soon. Already the horizon has begun to shift from black to gray. Judy takes her husband's hand and leads him down the hill, along the short path between ancient trees, back to the car. She puts him in the passenger seat, and gets behind the wheel.

"There was something about tonight," Edward says as she begins to drive home. "A feeling. I really thought they would come."

Judy pats his hand, takes it in her own, kisses his fingertips. "I know," she says. "But not tonight."

The first time Edward told her his story, he was hesitant, afraid she'd laugh, run off, tell him to lose her number. They had been dating about a year then, and in the years since, all forty-six and counting, she's heard the story so many times that she sometimes feels like she was there. Recent years have loosened Edward's tongue and now he'll tell anyone who will listen. Though these days, that's mostly Judy herself.

It started, of all places, at Woodstock. He and three friends drove up from Lackawanna, part of the small contingent that actually bought tickets ahead of time. Edward watched the first day, and was making his way back to the tent he was sharing with his buddy Roger after Joan Baez's set, a little after two in the morning. Slightly stoned, but mostly just wiped from a day in the heat, all of a sudden he was overcome by a powerful urge to leave, coupled with a clear vision of a hilltop surrounded by paper-white birch trees. Seemingly of their own volition, his feet led him away from the festival, away from the field and crowd. The commotion of laughter and debate and hushed love-making faded as he made his way toward the woods, then through them, following a tug in his brain like there was a hunk of magnetized metal in there, pulling him sharply forward. No one tried to stop him or even questioned him as he left.

Later, when he looked on a map, he learned that he'd walked for nearly seven miles, passing through working farms and fallow fields, over streams and train tracks. Eventually and suddenly, the fog over his brain lifted and he found himself on the top of tree-covered hill. A small circle was clear of foliage, and he stood there, his wits returning, beginning to panic about what he'd just done and how he'd get back. It would have had to be sometime around four in the morning if he walked at a good clip, but back then he was in fine shape and easily could cover that sort of ground in two hours. The night was cloudy, and just a hint of moonlight lit the area.

Until the UFO appeared. A bright flash of light and a bone-rattling hum. Branches snapped off of nearby trees, and maple leaves and pine needles floated to the ground like snow. Edward's body felt transmuted to something denser than flesh and yet lighter than air. Over the years, Judy has tried to imagine what this felt like, both rooted to the ground yet tugged skyward. She's not sure she will ever really know the feeling.

For a moment, the UFO hung above Edward's solid, static body, round and glowing, red and white lights blinking in an inscrutable rhythm. Then, like a cork from a bottle, Edward detached from the ground and shot up.

After that his memory gets hazy. Lying on a slab, bathed in light, surrounded by small gray beings with massive eyes and no mouths. But there's nothing painful in his recollections, no tests or probes, and he doesn't appreciate the jokes about that. What he remembers is a feeling of serenity, something approaching enlightenment. If the aliens had let him stay for just a bit longer, he thinks he might have transcended himself, become something more than merely human. Then there was an orange flash, and he was standing in the clearing, looking east at the first rays of morning. Eventually he gathered himself enough to wander to the nearest road and hitch back to Lackawanna.

When his friends got back themselves and asked where he'd gotten off to, Edward told them. He didn't think twice about it. Those days, there were a lot of out-there stories and beliefs circulating, and an alien abduction was hardly the craziest. Still, they laughed. He clammed up about it for a long time, but never stopped thinking about it.

The first time he shared all this with Judy was when she realized that he really and truly loved her. He proposed two weeks later, and of course she said yes.

Coffee tickles Judy's senses and draws her up from sleep later than usual the next morning. She hasn't used or needed an alarm in years. Most days, the days when Edward doesn't wake her with his nocturnal excursions, she wakes shortly after sun-up. Today, the sun is high and bright and hot, and Judy still feels she could sleep another two hours. But she gets up, steps into her slippers, and heads down the hall to the kitchen.

Edward sits at the kitchen table, a mug of coffee and the morning's paper in front of him, pen in hand and brow furrowed as he works his way through the crossword. He looks up as Judy enters. "Good morning." He stands to get her coffee, splashes in cream. Sheepish, not meeting her eye. Not an explicit apology, but after being together for this many years, Judy catches every nuance in his morning greeting, the gentleness with which he hands her the steaming mug.

"There were pine needles on the soles of my feet this morning," he says. "Thank you."

Judy sips her coffee, pats Edward on the elbow as she crosses around him, pulling a chair next to his own. He sits down next to her.

"Jaws," Judy says, pointing at the paper. "Nineteen down."

"Of course," Edward says as he pens it in. "Remember we saw that two days before going to the Cape for vacation? Not our best idea."

She laughs. "Definitely not."

Minutes pass, they drink coffee, fill in crossword boxes. A pleasant morning. More and more since they've retired, days seem to follow this pattern. That Judy wakes in the night, that Edward waits for aliens that may never come, that Judy tries to will herself to believe.

Judy won't bring it up. She doesn't anymore. There's no point.

"It seems crazy now," Edward finally says, his eyes on the puzzle. "When I'm out there, it makes so much sense, but in the light of day..."

She tries to put herself in his shoes, she really does. To want something so much, to feel that sort of compulsion. But she can't. She has what she wants.

"I just want you to be happy," she says softly. "I just want to make you happy."

"You do make me happy."

"I know." She looks into the dregs of her coffee. "Do you want a warm up?" She starts to stand, but stops when she feels Edward's hand on her hip.

"You make me happier than I've ever been. The... what happened to me is something I can't explain, the need to go to them. It's powerful. But I hope you know how important you are to me. More important than they could ever be."

"I know," Judy says. She smiles at him, gets them both more coffee. She's just a woman, one of billions. He's woken up with her countless times, slept next to her countless times, whispered and kissed and nuzzled. The aliens came only once and they changed his life. Why wouldn't he want to see them again?

Two nights in a row. Rare that Edward leaves two nights in the same week, let alone one right after the other. Judy cries when she reaches over and feels the empty space where her husband should be.

Slowly, she performs her routine check. Bathroom, living room, kitchen. All empty. She wipes her eyes, takes a deep breath, removes her keys from the ring, slips on her shoes.

When she opens the car door, the dome light pops on, and Judy jumps, practically has a heart attack. Sitting in the passenger seat, seatbelt already buckled, is Edward.

"Maybe you can come with me?" he says. "Maybe they'll take us both."

She doesn't laugh, doesn't shake her head disdainfully and try to coax him back to bed. She looks him up and down, his pleated navy blue pants, the business casual maroon polo shirt, the buffed brown shoes. She feels under-dressed.

Smiling for worrying about what she's wearing, Judy gets into the car. "Why not?" she says as she starts the engine. "Tonight could be the night."

Insects whirr and a breeze whistles through the fir trees. Moonlight dapples Judy and Edward as they stroll hand in hand down a dirt path to the hilltop. She's never really noticed how pretty it is here, how serene.

When they first stepped onto the path, Edward sped up, trying to tug her ahead, but Judy kept her pace steady, and Edward matched her. Now they walk like they did when they were first dating, like there's no destination. She wishes they could turn down one of the side paths, hike down some barely-marked trail, meander through the woods forever. But she lets Edward steer her until they reach the clearing. His clearing.

That looks different too, walking into it when it's empty. The stars twinkle above, the trees form a canopy that's almost a dome. Put together, it reminds her of when she visited the planetarium with her third grade class, how she looked up at the constellations dotting the ceiling as the guide pointed them out, outlines illuminating one by one.

"Which direction will they come from, do you think?" she asks, unaware that she planned to speak until after the words leave her lips. "Are they coming from a particular star?"

Edward beams. She's never asked him this question. "That one," he says, pointing to a constellation she doesn't recognize, an off-kilter box and swoop. "I think. I remember seeing it when they had me, and I got a warm feeling, a home feeling."

"That's a good way to feel," Judy says. Their hands detached at some point, but she takes his again. Together, they look up at the stars scattered like a child's toys.

Edward squeezes her hand. "I'm glad you're here."

She squeezes back. "Me too."

Under the wide and crowded sky, Judy and Edward stare upward and wait for the aliens to come back and take them away, to usher them into the future, to tell them the secrets of the universe.

"Sundown on the Hill" originally appeared in *Metaphorosis* on Friday, 31 March 2017

About the author

Timothy Mudie has never been to Woodstock or been abducted by aliens. He lives with his wife outside of Boston, where he works as an editor for a general interest publishing house.

Business As Usual

N.R. Lambert

"Thank you for registering with NamMo.com, America's

🦋 1 personalized munitions retailer..."

The message arrived at 8:46 a.m. Andy was fixing his coffee for the drive to work when the alert dinged. He finished stirring and sat at the counter before flipping open his hybrid and tapping the tablet's screen.

"Thank you for registering with NamMo.com, America's 🦋 1 personalized munitions retailer. As required by Section 80166 of the Violent Crime Control and Law Enforcement Act of 2026 (18 U.S.C. 1214 (d)), "Vicki's Law," we are informing you that a .45 ACP bullet was recently purchased, personalized with your name, on Tuesday, April 20th at 8:45 a.m.

"As a reminder, we are only required to notify you of the date and time of the purchase. Federal privacy laws prohibit the release of any additional information, including the name of the purchaser or the state in which it was purchased. Please bear in mind that while our custom products are live ammunition, the purchase of a personalized item does not constitute a threat and should not be perceived as one. NamMo Corporation and its employees are not responsible for the use, misuse, or transmission of personalized products after the purchase.

"This is an automated message, please do not reply. For questions, please contact customer service."

The site forced Andy to navigate a gauntlet of FAQs before the customer service page would direct him to any actual useful information.

We cannot release information...despite rare anomalous events...no reason for alarm...multiple U.S. residents with similar or the same name...not liable... NamMo Corp. does not endorse or promote the use of NamMo personalized products for the purpose of intimidation, threat, or harassment.

Did you find the answer to your question?
No.

Would you like to chat with a customer service representative?
Yes.

Finally, the site revealed an 800 number. An automated voice, warm and a little husky, answered after the first ring and reminded Andy that most questions could be answered by visiting the FAQ page of NamMo.com. Then the voice, which he dubbed "Mama NamMo," launched into a list of available automated options.

When he'd registered for the Vicki's Law notifications, Andy had never thought about actually getting one. At the time, it felt like a responsible thing to do and forget about, like signing up for one of those credit protection programs. It was weird to actually get an alert, but it would be a funny story and—Andy was sure—fertile soil for a lot of wise-ass comments at the office later.

"If you'd like to speak to a NamMo representative, please say, 'I'd like to talk to a representative.'"

Andy rolled his eyes and over-enunciated, "I'd like to talk to a representative."

"Okay, I'll connect you to a representative. One moment please."

Heavily muzacked Nirvana kicked in.

Why did his chest feel so tight? There were probably hundreds of Andy Wrights in America, even more globally. Statistically speaking, it was improbable that this had anything to do with him. Like NamMo said in their FAQ—was he really quoting the FAQ now?—there were "a myriad of reasons and occasions" for which someone might buy personalized bullets. NamMo.com even sold "handsome, hand-carved display cases" in a "stunning array of sizes and finishes," and offered "boundless custom options" that would allow the "simultaneous display of a photo, certificate, or trophy with the personalized bullet." Maybe some other Andy Wright had just finished boot camp, or made sharpshooter on his high school rifle team...

The music stumbled as Mama NamMo cut in to inform Andy that due to an unusually high call volume, his wait time would be approximately fifteen minutes. He glanced at the clock and popped open a chat channel with his cube-mate at Viance, an integrated telephonics tech company that specialized in "customer service solutions," including AI personalities like Mama.

hey, running late
everything okay?
yeah on hold with nammo.com
uh-oh, placing an order? should we be worried? lol!
ha. no, got a VL alert, I'm pretty sure it's just a glitch
there are probably a million of you getting the same msg right now
yeah, definitely
but I'll make sure we stick an intern up at reception just in case lol!

Andy cringed and started to reply, but his email chimed again. A new message from NamMo.com, probably to tell him that the whole thing was a big mistake.

"Thank you for registering with NamMo.com, America's ★1 personalized munitions retailer. As required by Section 80166 of the Violent Crime Control and Law Enforcement Act of 2026 (18 U.S.C. 1214 (d)), "Vicki's Law," we are informing you that a .45 ACP bullet was recently purchased, personalized with your name, on Tuesday, April 20th at 9:03 a.m."

If it weren't for the new time stamp in the alert, Andy would have thought it was a duplicate message, a bug in the automated notification system, which sent the messages out within a few seconds of purchase. He'd ask the rep about this one too, if he ever escaped hold purgatory, which now featured a string quartet deconstructing "Paranoid Android." Andy drummed his fingers along with the staccato bass line for a moment, then swiped open a browser and Googled his name.

Sure enough, dozens of Andy Wrights popped up in the results. He scrolled through, looking for a military dude or a high school kid. It was somewhat comforting to see all these other Andys. He assumed they'd all received the same alerts; at least the ones who'd registered for them after Vicki's Law passed.

Mama NamMo pierced the cello solo.

"NamMo Corporation's high quality personalized products make perfect keepsakes and souvenirs that will be treasured by your family for generations. Ask about our same-day delivery to make sure your gifts *always* arrive on time. NamMo Corporation is not responsible for the use, misuse, or transfer of NamMo products."

Andy recalled when NamMo first launched. Actually no, to be more precise, what he recalled was the moment he'd become aware that NamMo existed—that office massacre in Ohio. Not the Layton one, the Sumnerville one. That guy who bought ammo bearing each of his coworkers' names—every coffee-sharing, email-forwarding, birthday cake-cutting, cubicle-dwelling colleague, arranged together in a velvet-lined, handcrafted, custom cherry wood box.

Then, after, arranged together again in the parking lot, in plastic-lined, mass-produced body bags that the Sumnerville EMTs had to borrow from neighboring counties because their piecemeal volunteer station just didn't have enough on hand.

you still on hold?

yeah, just got a second alert, definitely a glitch or something

must be

anyone else there get an alert?

not that I know of, why?

Mama NamMo punctured Lite Inch Nails to remind Andy that NamMo's personalized products also made great holiday gifts.

"Are you kidding me?" Andy couldn't help it, even though he knew no one was listening. Hadn't anyone vetted the hold scripts? Did they just not care?

you're not going to believe this, one of the hold msgs: "nammo makes great holiday gifts"

the fuck? srsly, that's messed up.

right?

There was no way NamMo had forgotten, but obviously they'd hoped (or expected) that everyone else would. Vicki's Law wouldn't exist if it hadn't been for a "holiday gift," the so-called "Santa Slaughter."

After Sumnerville—or maybe it *was* Layton—NamMo bullets became *the* trendy gift for edgy celebrities, a punchline for late-night talk show hosts, and occasionally, a prank for teens with too much expendable cash. But then, around the holidays that same year, a guy in Newton, not *that* Newton—different guy, different Newton—bought pairs of customized bullets bearing the names of his ex-wife, his two estranged sons, his ex's new husband, and their infant daughter, Vicki.

He sent one of each pair, carefully wrapped, to his ex's house on Christmas Eve. Then, he showed up early on Christmas Day to deliver the matching bullets personally. He posted images of the slaughter on his feed, then shot himself with a single, impersonal bullet. The rabid, practically gleeful, media coverage reinvigorated public outrage toward NamMo Corp.

Mama interjected again; Andy's expected wait time was now less than four minutes.

less than 4!

lucky you! listen Naomi wants to go over the deck for tomorrow

shit, yeah, I'll follow up when I get in

k, good luck

thx

After the vigils, the thinkpieces, the thoughts and prayers, there was finally, *finally,* some action. "Vicki's Law." Originally, it was set up so that NamMo Corp. would be required to notify everyone who registered, and their local police precinct, that a bullet purchase in their name had been made, when and where it was made, and by whom. There was even a built-in wait period for delivery. Millions of Americans signed up for the service. But before it rolled out, the NRA got to work. Leaning heavily on privacy acts, they got Vicki's Law sanded down until it was as small and useless as a child's wooden toy coin.

The email chimed again. A new purchase alert, this one for 9:30 a.m.

Three?

A slow, cold panic pushed up from his gut and into Andy's chest. According to Mama NamMo, there was only one caller ahead of him. His coffee, forgotten, was a cold still life, caught in a weak sunbeam on the counter.

His email issued another gleeful chime. A new bullet. 9:31 a.m.

It had to be intentional. Why else would anyone buy one bullet at a time, when the site obviously allowed bulk purchases? If it was for a magazine's worth, the buyer could have bought them all in a single order. But to do it this way, one by one? Someone, somewhere was definitely trying to send a message to one of the Andy Wrights...

Andy didn't think he had any enemies. Then again, had any of the Sumnerville 33 expected their quiet, Rush-loving comptroller to—

A car door slammed outside.

Another ding.

"...We are informing you that a .45 ACP bullet..."

There was that one guy from Viance sales. Michael? Matthew? Always got way too aggressive during the inter-company softball games. One time, he and Andy had shared some heated words at the bar after a game, during which a tiny cup of ketchup might or might not have been dumped on Mike/Matt's head. But that certainly wouldn't justify something like this, would it? Besides that bar thing was years ago, no way Mike/Matt would still—

"Thank you for calling NamMo.com. This is Casey, how can I assist you?"

Andy was so used to Mama NamMo's smooth, but not-quite-sultry voice, that the perky, pipsqueak drawl of the rep made him jump a little.

"Hi, um, so I keep getting these notifications and I think maybe there's a glitch or something."

Casey waited a beat. A tactic Viance also taught its customers' fleets of reps, but usually one reserved for hostile callers. Her power pause was punctuated by the ding of another notification arriving.

"Okay sir, I can look into that for you, can you give me your name and account number please."

"Sure. It's Andy Wright. I don't have an account."

"Okay, Mr. Wright, I'm happy to assist you. What's the problem?"

"I keep getting these notifications about bullets personalized with my name, like I've gotten five or six now, and I think there might be a glitch." He didn't recognize his voice, taut and sharp as piano wire.

"Okay, Mr. Wright. Let me take a look." She tapped some keys and for a few moments, there was only the faint, steady sound of her breathing. Andy took a deep breath. His chest felt even tighter.

"Hmmm. Let's see." More tapping. "Okay sir, nothing to worry about."

Andy exhaled hard. He knew it had to be an error. But then Casey continued.

"There's no glitch, the notification system is working just fine. Those messages all correspond to actual purchases of NamMo personalized products."

"But, I've received," Andy quickly counted the emails, "six notifications in the last hour."

"Yep, that's correct Mr. Wright. I'm showing here that those correspond to six separate product purchases. Can I help you with anything else today or will that be all?"

"I mean...just...who would want this many bullets with one person's name?" Andy's thoughts touched on that guy down the hall who was always leaving enraged notes on neighbors' cars about their "shitty" parking jobs or hyperarticulate missives tacked to the cork board about the "increasingly pressing issue of sustained dog barking in our building." Was he the kind of guy wh—

"Sir, privacy laws restrict us from releasing information about the identity of our customers." Andy's head started to throb.

Another chime.

"But isn't there a limit? Like when do you start investigating? There has to be a level where it triggers some sort of 'suspicious activity' alert, right?"

Even before she replied, Andy sensed Casey's chipper attitude turning into something far steelier.

"Sir, NamMo Corp. is not responsible for the use, misuse, or transfer of our products."

"Wait. Are you serious?" Andy shouted, knowing immediately that it was a tactical error. At Viance, they would have trained Casey to end the call at that point. But he could still hear her breathing.

"Sir, I have to ask you to calm down. There are many reasons and occasions for which people purchase NamMo's personalized products. There is no cause for alarm."

A new message. New purchase. 9:43 a.m.

"That's eight!" Andy knew he sounded hysterical and a small part of him marveled that Casey hadn't yet terminated the call. "I mean, shouldn't you at least tell the police?"

"Sir, we encourage you to do what makes you feel comfortable. But we're not legally responsible for notifying law enforcement agencies about the purchase of our personalized products, nor can we release additional information to the authorities without a federal warrant..."

Andy barely heard her. His thoughts were scattered and skipping in all directions, like a handful of dried beans spilled on a hard tile floor. He closed his eyes and pinched the bridge of his nose. His mind spun through the zoetrope of possible candidates: That one IT guy who glared at everyone and never spoke. The boyfriend of that assistant he'd flirted with at the company party last year. That random internet dude who'd filled Andy's feed with streams of threats and gory images for weeks after Andy posted a mildly political opinion about an upcoming election. The possibilities blurred, a bright orange streak of panic running through his entire life.

"Sir? Did you have any other questions today?"

Andy opened his eyes. Several floors down he heard his building's front door slam shut. Probably just the mailman...or an equally late neighbor. But he stood to check the locks on his apartment door anyway. Then he sat again, though slightly further from the door than before.

"Sir?"

"Yes. Okay, but isn't there some kind of protocol, just in case?" Andy tried to keep his voice calm, but he could barely squeeze out the words. "I mean...should I go to work today? Or is that the last place I should go?"

Unless someone was planning on coming to his apartment? Maybe it would be safer to drive around for a while. But then, what if someone was waiting for him in the garage? Was anyone actually watching the security camera footage?

"Sir, if safety is a concern for you," Casey tapped a few more keys as she spoke, "I've just been authorized to offer you a special discount on a NamMo custom personal security package."

"No. No. I don't want that. I just want to know who's doing this. I want to know why!" Andy's shirt was heavy with sweat.

"Mr. Wright, as I mentioned earlier, I am legally restricted from violating our customer's privacy." Casey let the silence hang between them. Andy's breathing felt forced.

"But what am I supposed to do now?"

"Well sir," she was bright again, her allotted time with him was winding down; Andy could practically see the countdown clock on her monitor, "we suggest you go about business as usual. If you find that the notifications are disruptive, you can unsubscribe at any time by simply clicking on the 'unsubscribe' link at the bottom of the message."

Andy imagined Casey sitting in a white, brightly lit room—sterile, secure, safe. Just like the faceless "craftsmen" who right now were etching his name into metal over and over again, the shipping team who would soon pack boxes with personalized dread and send them to a stranger. He imagined the sharpened smiles of NamMo sales reps as they flaunted their hollow samples at gun shows and shooting ranges; the practiced grimaces of puppet politicians blanketing the country with their thoughts and prayers like junk mail. He thought about all the fingers that would touch those bullets, his bullets. The same ones that had held Vicki's bullet, before, and hadn't faltered—not even for a moment—after.

"Sir, have I answered all your questions today?"

Another chime. Andy tapped the mute toggle on his screen.

"Sir?"

"No. Not at all."

"I'm sorry to hear that. After this call, you're invited to complete the NamMo Corp. customer satisfact —"

Andy disconnected. A new email notification drifted down from the toolbar, somehow more ominous in its silent descent. 10:05 a.m. Andy stared at the screen for a long moment before reopening the chat channel.

hey, not going to make it in today
they can't keep you on hold forever dude LOL!
heh. let Naomi know too?
sure. no prob! see you tomorrow
thanks

Andy flipped the hybrid shut just as another alert ghosted across his screen. He stood, poured his coffee into the sink, and lingered there a moment before leaning forward to lower the blinds.

"Business as Usual" originally appeared in *Metaphorosis*
on Friday, 13 January 2017

About the author

N.R. Lambert grew up in New York City and learned early to avoid the empty subway car. Her writing has been published by *PseudoPod, Metaphorosis,*

Tor.com, TIME, LIFE, and *Entertainment Weekly.* In addition to her work as a pop culture author and copywriter, she volunteers with Read Ahead NYC, a reading-based mentoring program for elementary school students. She currently lives in Queens with her family and two saucy cats.

Look for very occasional updates at www.nrlambert.com.

Bad News from the Future

Angus Cervantes

"If you're really my future self," I said, "convince me."

"Because stopping time isn't convincing."

"I believe you have a time machine. Prove you're *me*." I tried again to straighten my head. "If you're me, you know how."

He smiled, sort of, anxious lines softening around his mouth. Would I become this sour-faced man? "And I know you've thought this through. Three secrets nobody knows."

"Now, only things I'd never tell any—"

"In the treefort with D'Arcy. What you threw in the library window. And that red-haired girl from choir."

"Ouch," I said. I wasn't talking, not exactly, but he could hear me. "Okay, I wish I'd forgotten those."

"Never did." He rubbed the purple scar across his forehead. Since I couldn't look out the windscreen of the van, I kept looking at him. At myself. I should smile more, or my two happy twins would grow up to be worried children. Smile more...parents have strange responsibilities.

"So," he said, "do you believe me now, or should I mention the red sports bag you hid—"

"You're me," I said, too loud, and he stopped. "So—huh. So we did it. We invented time travel—well then, listen, about the friction battery..."

"You stop working on that today," he said. "Just time travel, from now on. And it takes you ten more years."

"Wait," I said. "Should you tell me details like that? What about paradox? If I stop trying because I can't fail—if I do that, would I fail?"

He reached to touch the scar again, then lowered his hand with a jerk. "You won't fail, and you won't stop trying. As long as you believe me, you will keep trying." He glanced into the back seat, where the twins were safely buckled into their little seats.

"Believe you what?"

"It's complicated," he said, and took a deep breath. "Look, this is very bad news—"

"Oh, no," I said. Something went cold inside my belly, and I tried to close my eyes. They didn't move; I kept staring at his ugly, sad face. "Bad news from the future. What could possibly...?"

"You're having a car accident," he said, "The girls both die."

"No," I said. I couldn't breathe. I didn't have to breathe, in a frozen, unmoving moment stuck out of time, but I still needed air. "You can't let—we have a *time machine.*"

"I know we do. That's why I built it. Will build it."

"Ok," I said. "Got it. I'll stop the van. Switch off the —let me move—"

"It's too late," he said, and leaned back. "That bus there, behind me, it doesn't stop."

"No, look—" The bus' turn light was on. The driver's eyes were wide open. Wide, wide open. He looked helpless. Like he had just realized what was going to happen and couldn't do anything about it. "It's signalling."

"But it's not *stopping*. The front of this van shears right off, and I survive." He looked into the back seat. "But the girls *don't*."

"So pull them out—" I started, then stopped. "Time machine. You could have come ten minutes ago, in the driveway."

"No, I couldn't. I can't change what happens, self. The girls don't survive in this time. They don't."

"I'm turning the wheel," I said, and my voice was high—or whatever was making my voice in this timeless helpless moment. My arms didn't move, of course.

"Listen," he said. "This is what happens: they won't really die, because I'm taking them with me to the future."

My heart was still working. I heard it in my ears. Everything else was quiet and faded. "No," I said. "That won't work. Will it work?"

"It does work," he said. "And yes, I can prove it." He reached into his jacket for a picture, printed on a silver polymer, and he held it in front of my face. Ruthie and Jessie, maybe eight years old, longer in the face but so easy to recognize, so easy to love. They were running across a new backyard, laughing. A blurred adult figure after them, a dog. And the twins were happy. Alive.

The feeling—once I tried old-fashioned bungee jumping, and it was the same feeling: free-fall terror, then a sudden jerk and twist and you're flying. Now I was still helpless, but flying free, not falling. All the the terror and the weight of the world, gone, and all I wanted —knowing my children will survive.

I could die now.

No—I couldn't die. I had to invent a time machine, so I could come back, to here and now, with a scar on my face, and save them.

I stared out at the street, the stop sign I'd rolled through, the double-length bus unmoving on Fairfield Road. My mind started working. "Wait. The girls are three years old right now. If you do save them, they're still three. But how old are they in this picture? How did you even get this?"

"In the picture," he said, "they're eight. It's from us. From five years in my future, fifteen years in yours. Of course I need to know that the rescue will work, or what's the point of building the machine? My future self came back to my lab, where I was, and he brought me this."

I looked at the silver family picture again, and his grimy, split-nail fingers, holding it in front of my face, obscuring the bus that was about to destroy everything in my life. "Just the one picture? Nothing else at all?"

"A message, I guess. Information, really—for me mostly but also for you." He shifted to look at me more directly, and I noticed the deep lines around his eyes. "We're gonna die of a stroke."

"That's awful," I said. "No. Wait. How could he know, if he's still alive—"

"He, and you, and I, have all known since just this second," said my future self. "Time travel causes brutal compression waves in the blood. Even one trip is dangerous. More trips are like Russian roulette, adding bullets every time."

"I don't—" I said. "I don't quite get it." The shape of the rest of my life was just there, in front of me, and I could nearly understand it.

Then I did, the whole cascade, just as future self explained it to me, just when he didn't need to. "Future-future self," he said, "dies—died—in the lab, on the day you become me. The moment I invent the time machine, he appears in the lab, with blood coming out his ear. Holding this picture, for me to bring back to you today. He knows he'll die and he comes anyway."

"God," I said. "There's no choice in all this. He comes anyway, and he dies?"

"He was still warm when I left," said the world's first time traveller, to the man who would become him.

My future self was bumping around in the back, spreading some metallic net over the matching purple carseats. I was alone in the front, unmoving as ever, staring helplessly at the frozen bus. My nose was running and I couldn't wipe it. "I want to talk to them."

"You will," he said from behind me. "In ten years. You'll get them back, self." A pause. "It's worth it." His voice cracked. "Ready?"

"Wait," I said. I sniffed to clear my nose. It didn't do a thing. "Okay."

A deep violet light flared in the mirror, and I pressed backward in my seat, straight through the stop sign, ahead of the bus, which wasn't stopping, coming into the side passenger door, tires really do screech, the driver's mouth wide open now, squeezing his eyes—"No," I said. I hadn't caught up with the process of what would happen—with the *implications*.

From the back seat, a tiny thunderclap. I started to turn my head.

The sound of the crash was deep and surprisingly hollow, like kicking a cardboard box.

Then I was spinning away, still strapped in, the front of the van ripped off. In flashes as I whirled: the fuel-cell ruptured and a cloud of gas ballooning like a toy into the air, then trees, then the bus again, then a broad *whumph* and flames and a spinning fragment of—

I woke up with a heavy fireman kneeling on me, silhouetted against a pyramid of flame and black billowing smoke. "No," he was saying. "Stay the hell down, mister."

"My girls," I said. My forehead was numb, and wet. "In the van. Two children. Let me go," I said. "Please. Children, two carseats—". Then I stopped, and thought carefully. "Did you get my children out of the van?"

The fireman blinked twice, and his jaw tightened. "I don't know," he lied. "But stay down."

Ten years, the man said.

"Bad News from the Future" originally appeared in *Metaphorosis*
on Friday, 17 March 2017

About the author

Angus Cervantes is a West Coast writer with a keen sense of nostalgia and a blurry vision of the future. He is working on designing new tenses for when time travel will have to be-en invent.

The Cure for Cancer

Ryan Fitzpatrick

The cure for cancer exists. It can be found in the Mato Grosso region of Brazil, an intertropical convergence zone in the heart of the country. Due to the minerals and nutrients blown in from both the North and the South Sea, the area is covered in a thick blanket of rainforest, making the region rich in a biodiversity that extends not only to flora and fauna, but to other, harder to classify biota.

The cure for cancer grows, when the conditions are right, in the cell membrane of a rare and specialised fungus, belonging to the class of Basidiomycota known as Polypores. The conditions for the fungus to reach maturity are extraordinarily singular, and contribute to its sparse numbers. For example, because the fungus is saprotrophic and seeks its nutrients from decaying matter, the fallen tree on which it grows must meet the following criteria; dry yet near water; sheltered from rain, but unobstructed from the suns rays for eleven of the twelve hours it gives in this part of the world; and outside of the borders of any Capuchin or Tamarin tribes, both of which have evolved to find the hymenium of the polypore to be something of a delicacy.

However, in a cruel twist of biological fate, the polypore cannot survive the journey through the intestinal tract of either of these species. The fungus has also not evolved to feature basidiospores, and as such, its spore dispersal is limited and localised.

Due to these facts, the entire colony of the unnamed polypore can only be found in a thirty centimetre circle on the bark of a fallen rosewood, sheltered by a tilted rock and tucked into a bend of one of the Rio Negro's many unmarked tributaries.

To extract the cure, the plant must be harvested approximately one week before it reaches maturity. The husk-like casing of the ruptured volva must then be picked, peeled, and dried, preferably under laboratory conditions to avoid contamination. However, open air drying would work too if necessity demanded it. Either way, this initial stage of the process can take between twelve and fifteen days, and visual indicators (a browning of the volva and a curling of the stem) will indicate when the fungi are ready for the next step.

When fully dried, the husks of the fungi should be removed and the remains discarded. The collected husks should then be crushed or blended into a fine dust and soaked in an aqueous solution of methylecgonidine. After three days (stored at room temperature in a dark space), the liquid should be passed through a neutral paper filter cloth to leave a dark, tea coloured liquid. It should be viscous in consistency.

The remaining mixture should be boiled at 95°C in sterilized equipment and the condensate collected and refrigerated. The mixture can then be administered intravenously in diminishing doses until the cancer is in remission. The remaining liquid can be ingested orally (either in pill or liquid form) or via transdermal patch. Long term use will complete the treatment, and the patient will be cancer free.

This is a relatively simple extraction process for medication, and although the conditions of the fungi's growth are rare in the wild, they are easily recreated in the lab. What's more, with only a few generations of selective breeding, the fungus could be made to be more potent and faster acting, making it a cheap and reliable source of continued good health for the 8.8 million sufferers of cancer per year.

But no man has yet discovered this, and it is possible that no man will.

A low rumbling sounds out across the landscape and birds scatter. It is the sound of gasoline combusting inside an engine.

A three-toed sloth moves sluggishly in the opposite direction, crossing the forest floor in a calculated but rare moment of risk. Her elongated claws, mottled as they were with patches of moss, lightly caress the group of fungi, knocking a few from the fallen trunk and into the mud. A few moments later and the sloth is gone, seeking refuge in the comparative safety of the tree tops.

If the sloth were sentient enough to be poetic, she might see the tree on which she now drowses as the mast of a sinking ship, the lookout for an ever diminishing life boat. In the distance – although not as distant as yesterday – the harvesters and forwarders continue their purge of the rainforest, pushing deeper, leaving behind them a wake of palm oil production.

The sloth closes her eyes, the buzzing of the far away machines lulling her into easy sleep. Beneath, predators and prey alike continue to cling to the lifeboat, battling for space as the walls close in around them. In the centre of it all, the Rio Grande, sometimes fast, sometimes slow, continues its unending journey. The cure for cancer awaits its fate.

"The Cure for Cancer" originally appeared in *Metaphorosis* on Friday, 1 December 2017

About the author

Ryan Fitzpatrick lives and writes in the UK.

The Lost Languages of Exiles

Laura E. Price

The shoes they gave her don't fit.

She notices in the waiting area of the IWT counseling office and holds one foot out in front of her. Wiggles her toes and feels them rubbing against the inside front seam of the shoe. It's felt like this since she put it on, but she's just now stopped long enough to really feel it. The shoe is canvas and rubber, a basic sneaker, and probably half a size too small. Does time dilation make your feet spread? Or did some tech somewhere type in the wrong shoe size in a rush?

She puts her foot back down. Now she notices the way both shoes encase her feet, pinching and rubbing in odd spots.

The only other person in the room with her is Harry, and he won't look at her. Harry's not looking at anybody, lately, except maybe *his* psychologist. He fidgets, leg bouncing and fingers drumming: the behavior mods would have kept him from that—the movement, the feelings making him do it—but they're off now. Everyone from their crew is edgy, scraping against one another in various ways. Her own tension runs all along the edges of her body, a tremor and spark of panic and irritation just at the tips of her fingers and ears and toes. She pushes her hands into her thighs, her toes into the seams of her shoes, exhales.

When they'd all stood frozen and staring at the skip-lagged face of the Admiral on the main viewscreen, Harry's fingers were the first things to move. They scrambled over the console and slammed the buttons down until the speakers let out a godawful screech and the Admiral's voice came through.

"—you've been gone five years, Captain. We thought you were all dead."

She leaves Harry in the waiting room when it's her turn. The office is dim, carpeted, furnished with big chairs and a desk shoved into one corner. Beach sounds play from speakers she can't find.

She sits in one chair and the psychologist sits in the other across from her, not at the desk, and they talk.

"How are you feeling?"

She's feeling the clothes she's wearing, now she's noticed the shoe. The waistband of her pants, the collar of her shirt against her throat. She has her left foot wrapped around her right calf, so her shoelaces dig into her pants, into her skin.

"I guess I feel … stunned? Slow. Half-blind—they aren't letting me access anything besides novels and old television shows right now." She'd seen half a news headline—*Exiled Imperator Poisoned in Bid to Consolidate*—and a sentence or so of the story under it. Her fingers tighten on the seams of her pants. She ignores the memory, focuses on her clothes.

"That's understandable," the psychologist tells her. Fran. She's pretty sure Fran's the one who wears glasses.

"Are they really retiring us all?" Lia asks. She crosses her arms low across her stomach, hooking her fingers into the waistband. "Before they blacked out the news, I saw that they were going to retire us?" She still has three years before her first opt-out. She can—could

—re-up twice more before retirement. After that she could apply for admin in the company.

"They are. Nobody knows what happened to you all out there. They don't want to take chances." Fran's eyes are steady on hers through her glasses. Even admin requires occasional space work.

"I don't ... know what to. I just." Lia stops, because she has no idea where that sentence will end.

"How old were you when you joined Inter-World Transport, Lia?"

"Twelve." Her father got the papers after he spent a night coughing up blood instead of the usual grayish phlegm that all the adults in their town had in their lungs.

"So you're twenty-four, now."

"I'm—" *Nineteen.* No. They were gone five years. It only felt like six months. She does the math in her head. "I guess I am, yeah."

"What had you planned to do, once your tour was up?"

"I was ... I'd assumed I'd. Um. Re-up. I don't tend to make plans past my next leave, really." She scrubs a hand through her hair, avoiding the ports behind her ears but rubbing around the one at the back of her head, which itches today. She'd had thoughts, about maybe finally taking some of the accumulated leave time she'd banked, if things went well with Ianto. She's never thought about any of *this.* Her heart speeds up as *twenty-four* echoes in her head; emotion floods her hands and fingers, fills her throat and sinuses. There's *too much* feeling and she doesn't want to drown in it; she wants to be able to *think.* She wants to be able to *breathe.*

She doesn't look at Fran, who says, carefully, watching her, "Well, you're here for the next three months. The company wants to run tests—psych and physicals, bloodwork, scans, that sort of thing—and ask you some questions about what you remember. They're also going to make sure you have some adjustment training—"

The panic eases at the boring company BS, recedes enough so that she can manage to look at Fran and ask, "*Do they* even know what that means?"

Fran grins in the cynical way that she and her shipmates do when discussing their employer; Lia's not sure if it makes her feel better or not. "I understand they're going to be contacting people who specialize in prisoner and military re-integration." Her grin softens into a smile. "They know this is unprecedented, Lia. They want to ease your transition as much as they can."

"I'm sure PR is breathing down Corporate's neck, as well."

"They lost a transport, sixty-two percent of which was manned by people they'd more or less bought as kids. It was a PR nightmare, even in the places that *don't* find IWT's various recruitment methods controversial."

Lia says nothing. There's nothing *to* say, really; she's glad she didn't starve to death or die from gray-lung before she turned sixteen, and this last trip was just another six-month tour for her. But Fran's voice saying *twenty-four* and *reports are unclear as to whether Rhydderch's companions were also* just before the screen went black won't leave her alone now. She grinds her foot into her calf, feels her shoelaces and the cloth of her pants against her flesh.

"Look," Fran says, "they didn't know why the *St. Cloud* disappeared, and now you're all back and they don't know why that happened, either—they just know all kinds of eyes are on them, yet again. The end result, though, is that they're going to try and help you." End results have long been the argument for Inter-World Transport: their motives may be self-serving, their tech may be ethically dubious, but they give the poor, the debtors, and the various people the world forgets the chance to become healthy, productive members of society. Plus, your cargo is delivered safely and on time by our always professional staff!

Fran's still talking. "Over the next weeks, think about what you want to do. Five years of back pay--you'll have money enough to live for a while before you need to work, but it's better to walk out of here with a plan than without one."

The first thing she remembers Ianto Couriseme saying was not to her, but to Meurig Rhydderch, the Imperator-in-exile of the Sovereign Bishopric of Laendris, on the planet Colophale. Which was now called Homshoi. The coup had been bloody and too intricate to follow when you spent six months at a time in deep space.

"It seems archaic, though—they own you until you're, what, ten years in?" Meurig had asked her one night in the mess hall, as they picked over the last bits of food on their plates.

Ianto, until now his Imperator's shadow, rolled his eyes. "You mean, archaic like generations of an entire family sworn to protect the royalty, whether they would or no?"

He was relaxed, slouched in a chair and leaning his head on an arm propped on the mess hall table, looking wryly at Meurig, who seemed self-deprecating but not particularly ashamed of himself. Ianto's grin caught and kept her eyes, even though the mods tempered her jolt of reaction to it. Meurig went on, "As archaic as keeping the youngest child as surety and sending the eldest into exile, I suppose. It sounds like a goddamned fairy tale, doesn't it?"

"If you cast it romantically, it's easier to live with," Lia said, and Meurig laughed, but Ianto gave her an odd, shadowed look before he smiled, slowly.

It takes forever before the Re-Assimilation Training is set up, and by then nearly all of the *St. Cloud*'s crew are restless, cut off from everything. That's not new; it's part of the job, but usually they're only six months behind, not five years. The company blocked the news sites two hours after the ship touched down—not quite soon enough to keep her from a search once she discovered she no longer had an email account, but fast enough to cut off the first news report she found after one sentence.

They've let them have family news, the ones who had family. E-mail, screened; new e-mail addresses because they purged all the *St. Cloud*'s crew's accounts two years ago. Dr. Quiroga's mother has cancer, is in the middle of treatment; Piotr's wife had their baby, and that baby is four. Lia, thinking about the solidity of family and the quake of losing five years with them, decides she's probably lucky. She doesn't think of fragile things, new connections, easily snapped when the ground convulses. Not much, anyway. Not really.

It's not all sad—Iona Kawa'iia's been stomping around mad that she saw spoilers for the end of *Bitumen Falls,* and now she can't access the show because they don't want them seeing anything that came out more recently than five years ago. And Jorge O'Malley got video of Captain Oshiro's reaction when his wife told him she'd sold his vintage skimmer, so they've all seen that one. It's not all sad. It doesn't all have to be sad.

"Your Laendish is very good."

Ianto fell into step with her as she walked from her station back toward her quarters. He wasn't that much taller than she was, and he had a loping sort of walk that he tried to restrain in order to keep pace with her. His hair was plaited into two braids that he wore looped at the back of his head, but curls kept escaping along the edges and sides. "Thank you," she said. "How's my accent?"

"Good. Possibly a little too posh—you sound like a queen in a film. But good." He smiled, a crooked grin, and went on, "You're the ship's linguist?"

"I'm one of them." The *St. Cloud* was mostly a freighter, rarely took passengers. She'd been the lucky lottery winner whose head was hastily stuffed with Laendris' dead-to-most-of-the-system language so that their last-minute additions could communicate with someone. The speed of the upload had been disconcerting; she'd dreamed in Laendish the night after the upload and woken up feeling ... off-balance. Unmoored.

"Can you, say, teach? Is that possible with the ports? I'm afraid I don't quite understand how they work ..."

"Nobody quite understands how the ports work," she said with a grin back at him. "But yes, I can teach, if I know the language. What are you looking for?"

"Could you teach me some English, before we dock? Maybe some Harekaans? Meurig seems to think he'll be fine knowing not a word of anything, but ... well, it *is* my familial obligation to take care of him. If you have time, of course, and if they're in your repertoire ..."

"Absolutely," she said, with professional smile and voice. "I'd be happy to."

There is bloodwork (lots of needles) and there are scans (full body, brain, random bits that make no sense, like her stomach and her right bicep, one of her hands). There are questions: her interviewer (whom she does not think of as an inquisitor, not at all) is a smiling, sandy-haired guy with a Harekaans accent and a dependence on his handheld. He's scrolling through something when she arrives.

"So you have no memory of anything out of the ordinary happening on this trip?" he asks, finally looking up from where he's been tapping notes onto the screen.

"Nothing. But I'm not bridge crew; I'm a cargo linguist. I spend most of my duty time belowdecks doing landing and retrieval prep, negotiating prices and permits in the native language; otherwise I'm pretty low on the need-to-know list."

"Why were you on the bridge when the *St. Cloud* returned?" he asks disinterestedly.

"Delivering a final inventory report to Captain Oshiro. The docs messaging system was down for maintenance, so I delivered it by hand."

"And during the trip there was nothing physical—no sudden lurching or shuddering at any point?"

She has a sudden image from an old television show, all the actors throwing themselves across the set of their sailing ship when some sort of sea monster rammed it. "No," she says, amused and quietly delighted to feel something good.

"No sudden ... um ... psychic disturbances?"

She couldn't figure out, at first, why she'd gone looking for Ianto when she wasn't on duty. It had felt strange; her mind had offered up *suffer a sea-change* to her, and maybe it had been apt: muted by the behavior mods they'd implanted in her limbic system, but huge, slow, seemingly inevitable.

She shakes her head, amusement gone, and that was the wrong trip, anyway. *That* trip, Ianto's trip, went without a hitch. "No, nothing like that," she says, and fights against the urge to seize his handheld and its open access when he props it up to start typing his report.

"How are you feeling?"

"Like half my brain is missing." She rubs her eyes, runs a finger hard around her ports where they itch and ache. "My languages are fading."

"All of them?" Fran asks.

It hurts in her chest to explain it; she wishes the mods were active so she could talk without her voice cracking as she counts on her fingers. "I've still got English and Portuguese, but they're native tongues. French isn't too bad, probably because of the Portuguese. Bilali's still mostly there, and maybe, I dunno, half of Harekaans and a quarter of Mandarin? I can still *read* Farsi, which seems completely counterintuitive. But the rest are ... they're like echoes. They sound familiar, but I just don't know."

"It makes sense. You haven't had any uploads, no refreshment."

"Yeah, I know, I just—languages are what I *do.* My brain is. Suited to it? They think, anyway, they say that shit but they don't *know.* I keep—what *good* am I, now? I'm not a pilot or a medic, I'm just a *linguist,* it's not like they need me anywhere else—"

"Well," Fran says her voice soothing, "There are certainly a number of things you can do with fluency in English and Portuguese, and some—what did you say? Bilali and Harekaans. We can explore some of them, too. But Lia, you have to remember that you're more than what you've done for IWT."

It's all true. It doesn't help, because it's true, but it isn't *all,* and she's not going to talk about the rest of it, about which language she's been trying to coax out of her stupid, regressing brain.

She takes a breath, hitches in the middle, wipes her face with the palm of her hand. This is ridiculous, mourning something she knew would happen, and *crying.* It's been weeks since they turned the mods off; everything should have settled by now, and she's not sure why it hasn't. "I didn't think it would hit me this hard," she says, then lets out a wet-choked laugh because *obviously.*

"So he's going to fire you once he's settled wherever it is he's going?" Books stacked neatly around them, the lesson abandoned for the day in favor of talking to each other, and Laendish easier for both of them.

"It's not that harsh," Ianto said, shaking his head at his hands. He sat tailor-style, his body's lines long, slender, a cascade of grace. He didn't look like anyone's idea of a bodyguard, but Meurig liked to tell stories at dinner about the part Ianto played during the coup and after it—assassination attempts foiled, the Imperator's uprisings. Sometimes, though, in his enthusiasm, Meurig stumbled into allusions to other things, and Ianto's body turned from flowing poise to elbows and knees and high shoulders, until Meurig speedily changed the subject. "Meurig feels a certain amount of guilt that I was sent with him, that I can't just go back after. He doesn't see it as firing; he sees it as freeing me from an obligation I had no say in accepting. Although he could always call me back, if they ever call him back."

"Do you think they will?" she asked.

"No. No, that government's ensconced for at least a generation or two." He grinned a twisted sort of grin that matched the bitter-philosopher tone of his voice.

When he didn't seem to want to continue that line of conversation, Lia asked, "And do you have plans for your forced semi-retirement?" She tried to sound light.

He shrugged. "I thought I'd live in the city? I can't imagine living in the countryside—I grew up in a city. Though the idea of an entire apartment to myself is *decadent.*" She nodded, let out a breathless laugh because it did. "I suppose I'll get a job. My money won't last forever." He grinned at her, crooked but not bitter, and asked, "Xiankin is your home port, isn't it?"

She grinned back at him; she couldn't seem to help but smile at Ianto when he smiled at her. It was disconcerting. "It is. We'll have five days' leave, then most of us are going back out for six months."

"So in six months, you could come see my apartment. Maybe have dinner?" He tilted his head so that he was smiling at her sideways.

She raised her eyebrows, hoping her expression told him that she knew exactly what he was doing with the coy looks and the playful tone. "I could," she said.

Harry sits down next to her in the dining hall. She's eating, reading *A Fisherman of the Inland Sea* on her handheld, debating in the back of her mind whether she ought to ask for a translation of it in Harekaans or Bilali to try and keep them up the old-school way.

Harry's doing better, if one can tell from a distance. Some days he's withdrawn, some days he's out of his own head and seems normal. Like today; he's actually looking at her.

They chat for a few minutes—two of the engineering crew are going to get married once they're released; Dr. Quiroga's mother is responding well to treatment.

"So, you make a plan yet for after we're out?" Harry asks her.

"No." She takes a breath, lets it out. "You?"

"Nah. Well, taking the money and running. Maybe go to Caszoeatu, hit some clubs, lay on the beach for a couple years."

"You have always been a hedonist, Harry, so this plan does not surprise me."

"They've owned me since I was eight years old; I may as well enjoy my unexpected freedom."

She snorts. Harry smiles at her. "So, Lia ..."

"Harry Das, you are *not* asking me to run away to Caszoeatu with you," she says with a laugh.

"No. I am propositioning you, though." He raises his eyebrows, lets his smile go from genuine to cheesy.

She thinks about it for a long minute. She and Harry used to hook up on leave all the time, during the first couple of days when the mods turned off and everyone was either mainlining sugar or fucking each other through the emotional overload. It was good, and they've always got along well enough. "Come on," he wheedles, "my therapist says it'll be good for my mental health."

She rolls her eyes and shoves him, watches him a little as she speaks. "Thanks, but no."

He takes it fine, she thinks. "You sure?"

"I am," she says, carefully. He squints at her.

"You got somebody else?" he asks, sly. He's always good at sniffing out a secret. Lia's just never had anything she cared about keeping to herself before. The problem is, she doesn't know how to answer without lying, at least a little, and thanks to the mods they're all awful liars due to lack of practice.

She settles for, "Kind of."

Harry keeps watching her and finally says, "It's that dude with the braids, trip before last." She doesn't respond, though her heart startles her with a heavy thud against her breastbone. "That sucks," he says. "I mean, is he still even around?"

"I don't know," she says; *reports are unclear as to whether.* She picks up her handheld and looks for her place. "And we're blacked out for who knows how long."

"Five years is a long time to wait for a hookup," Harry says. His tone is easy. His tone is always easy, but she curls her hand into a fist and digs her nails into her palm. They've long played this game of pushing and mocking; no matter how many times they've fucked, they've never really been intimate or vulnerable with each other, and she isn't starting now.

Lia forces airiness into her voice. "You should go ask Kawa'iia, she's always had a thing for you."

Now Harry rolls *his* eyes and stands up. "I do not need that giant vat of crazy opened, thanks. I will make do with my right hand or possibly proposition O'Malley."

Lia smiles, hopes it looks real. "He's cute—you should rank him higher than your hand."

"But he's in *session* and I'm *horny* ..." Harry fake-wails as he walks away. Lia watches him for three counted breaths before looking back at her book, waits until the doors close behind him and his footsteps fade before she puts the book down and buries her head in her hands.

Ianto kissed her. She wanted him to—something off-center and pale in her chest just *longed* for him to kiss her—but she ducked away before it was anything beyond a brushing of mouths together.

"Sorry," she said, "It's not me, it's the mods, I promise." She wished they shut embarrassment down as efficiently as they did lust. But when she looked at him, he was smiling at her. He took her hand, touched her knuckles one by one with his index finger until the embarrassment went away and she was left feeling a little breathless, a little lost, with that same tidal pull that sent her looking for him whenever she had the chance.

She gets herself off dozens of times to the memory of that sweet sweep of his mouth over hers. She remembers that and his scarred hands on her skin, the heat of his fingers against her knuckles, and it's better than all of the crazy-intense sex she used to have on leave.

But after, she thinks too much. Now the mods are off for good. The world is five years older. She doesn't know anything, really. Nothing that's happened in the news beyond that half a headline, which fills her head with *Poisoned* and *unclear,* setting her spinning through scenarios and what-ifs where Ianto is dead, where Ianto is shattered by the death of his Imperator, where Ianto is married or in love or in mourning and has left the city or the country or, hell, the entire planet, and she just wants to think of *anything* else, but what else is there to think of? The future she didn't realize was coming in the universe she's never really paid attention to beyond the languages of the people in it?

Eventually she falls asleep. She dreams in Laendish, wakes up, and spends the rest of the night trying to fall back into the dream.

About a week before their release into the world, their net access returns.

A bunch of them are in the lounge, talking, playing cards, watching old cartoons on the big monitors, and all of them have their handhelds with them. Lia's reading; she's always been one of the crew who didn't enjoy the close quarters they'd been stuck with, but lately she just wants people around, if not talking directly to her.

Harry's pocket lights up and buzzes, then O'Malley's and Kawa'iia's, then a few more, right in a row. *Everyone* gropes for their devices. Lia closes out of her book and stares at her screen, as though that will make the net come back faster.

It lights up in her hand, vibrating, flashes a "connecting" message at her that disappears again before her heart has a chance to slow down. Harry makes a happy affirmative noise; O'Malley, who has loudly enjoyed their exile from the 'nets, groans. The room fills with the pings and clicks and muffled swearing that comes with people setting up new tech, connecting their new email accounts; Kawa'iia lets out a triumphant, "*Yes,* I can download the last four Kilkennan books!" and Harry asks her, "He didn't die before he finished the series?"

Finally a message emerges from the swirl of colors undulating on her screen: *Hello, Lia, what would you like to do today?*

Her hands shake as she logs onto the news nets.

Ianto smiled at the card in his hand, the smile that emphasized how crooked his nose was, and said, "I've not even got a device yet. I'll have to remedy that as soon as I'm allowed."

"Send me e-mail when you do. I won't get it until I get back, but at least I'll be able to find you for dinner."

He shifted back from her on the mats—yoga and tai chi this time as an excuse to sit and talk—and said, voice much younger than usual, "You don't have to, you know. I won't—well, I'll be upset, but. If you find that it's not ... with the mods off, if you find you don't ..."

"I can tell how I feel," she said.

"Still," he said, and brushed her knuckles with his fingertips.

"Still," she said. "I'll contact you, no matter what, okay? In six months. Make sure you have a handheld."

On the day they're released, she takes a bus downtown and goes shopping. A new shirt—black tank top with an umbrella in a circle on the front that she likes the look of—and new shoes that just slip on. As she pays for it all with her handheld the cashier tells her, with a nod to the shirt, what a great band they are.

"This is a band?" she asks, immediately losing the cashier's interest. Clearly, she's a dilettante in the world of music. As she changes her shirt and shoes in the bathroom of a coffee shop, she just hopes the Rainmakers are a band she'd like if she heard them.

It's not like she's been released from prison, she reflects. It's not even like she's a new immigrant—this is a major IWT hub, one of four in the system, and the largest employer in this country, possibly on this planet. Corporate has offices here; warehousing; cargo processing; intake for voluntaries and indentureds; training for plebes and leave for vets; a quarter of IWT is based out of Xiankin. She's been here before, lots of times, though the last time was ... well, months ago or years, depending. She knows where things are, she knows how to get to them, she knows where and how to find transport and how the money works. She even knows where the road construction is, since apparently it hasn't progressed more than a block in five years.

What's different is that she doesn't need to check to see how much time she has left before she has to get back to base. She could go anywhere. Stay there as long as she wants. Nobody would come looking for her. Nobody could, since she didn't give them a new address. Fran had pushed her for one, but Lia couldn't tell her because Lia doesn't *know*. It's the first time in her life she hasn't known where she'll be sleeping, just that she has the money to decide later.

That much freedom makes her feel lightheaded, light-stomached, so she sits on a transport station bench to catch her breath.

The metal is warm under her. It feels good, baking through her clothes. The street is busy: it smells of fumes from the vehicles that pass by—the older ones loud and rumbling, the newer ones buzzing or humming —and food from the restaurants that are just beginning to open up for lunch. Horns honk and people talk, either into their handhelds or to each other in person; she hears ring tones and the chirping sounds of calls being made; snippets of conversations in different languages, some of which she can understand, some she can't.

The city is always busy this time of day. She has always wondered if people actually work in offices here, or if there's some sort of job that involves just walking around in business attire. There are IWT plebes with red-rimmed implants and newly-shorn hair walking clumped together and stiff in their uniforms with a couple of vets, younger than they are, who must be showing them around. They all glance at her, then away, then back fast when they register her ports and civilian clothes. Maybe they know what crew she's from, maybe not—she scowls at them, command-face, and they hurry off. The civilians don't really pay attention to her, just a glance now and then like you'd glance at anyone sitting on a bench in the middle of the day. They're used to the IWT by now, whether or not they approve of it.

The fact that she has not, actually, planned anything past getting new clothes is not the only thing keeping her from breathing. She looks at her handheld, suddenly all strange angles and edges against her palm in her hand. Her search of the news nets gave her fewer answers than she'd hoped: Meurig poisoned and dead dominated two days' news three years ago, with just one sentence in one article brushing near Ianto's existence, let alone anything else. *Initial reports are unclear as to whether Rhydderch's companions were also part of the plot to assassinate him, and if he had, as accused by the Honshoi Imperator, actually established a 'court-in-exile' on Xiankin.*

That's as far as she's gotten.

She pulls her feet up under her on the bench. The city stretches out around her; the world stretches out beyond that. She doesn't know anything about the future, and it scares her breathless, but she knows what she wants to do. So she types *Ianto Couriseme* into the search bar.

Three steps down the gangplank, another four through the gate, and all the mods shut off at once.

It felt like simultaneously uploading the Oxford English Dictionary and the Royal Dictionary of The Feudal Republic of Bilal—it swamped her, made her lose her moorings.

It was so much more than the usual horny-happy-excited-reckless swoop of feelings unfettered; she could barely see through this to get to her quarters—thank god the retinal scans could work through tears—and she sobbed as she thought of him walking away from her with his exiled Imperator into the city, sobbed far more than probably she should have, but things always felt like *more* right after the mods shut off; all you could do was ride it until it settled.

Five days of leave. She spent them looking for him without expecting to find him—too soon for them to be registered and logged, not with how covertly they had been travelling—but hoping she could tell him that she would see him when she got back.

She didn't find him.

It was all right. She'd find him after this next tour. Six months, less a week, she'd find him and knock on his door.

After fifteen minutes of searching, there's a phone number on the screen. And an address.

She doesn't touch the number. Instead she pulls up the GPS program.

This is really, really stupid.

Her knuckles sting from knocking at the red door of this brick townhouse. It's on a quieter street. Residential. She gets the feeling, from the colors of the doors and curtains, the decorations on the porches and in the tiny front yards, that this is mostly an immigrant neighborhood. It's nice. It feels friendly and looks lived-in, like people have put down roots here. But she's still so terrified she can barely breathe. Part of her, exasperated, hopes to god that the longer she's off the behavior mods, the easier it will be to cope with some of these emotions.

The door opens, and there he is.

She can't talk for a minute, or breathe; she's too busy looking at him. He's *here*.

He hasn't changed very much at all. He was twenty-one when she saw him last, so he must be twenty-six now; his hair is shorter, not braided—it's a mass of curls. His eyes are still hazel, his nose still crooked, his skin still light brown. And his smile still takes up half his face, once it manages to spread out completely.

He says something in Laendish that ends with a soft, astonished, "Lia."

"I ... um. Hello." She says it in English, smiles back at him, feeling slightly drunk. She runs her hand over her head and looks sideways, quickly, just to have a minute where she's *not* looking at him, so she can collect her thoughts or take a breath or something, but then her eyes are pulled right back to him. "I ... I can't speak Laendish anymore—it's faded out. I don't know if you knew—"

"Everyone thought you were all dead." His accent is lilting and lovely. He frowns a little and reaches out one hand to touch her shoulder.

The feeling of his hand on her skin stills her; he's warm and right in front of her. She probably should have waited to come here until she had things better under control. Although, at this point, she thinks that might have been never.

"We can speak English," he says. "I have a little Portuguese, too, but not much." His hand leaves her shoulder, but stays in the air between them for a second. He takes a step out onto the stoop. "Are you—you actually *found* me," he said, his voice pitched high and disbelieving. "When I heard your ship came back, I rather—" He stops, takes a deep breath, and she braces herself for something she won't want to hear.

And then he asks, in a quieter, smaller voice, "Please tell me—you are here to stay with me, Lia?"

"I'd like to," she says. There's a slow surge of current rushing through her—head and arms and legs; ears and fingers and toes—she looks down at her new shoes, bright white in the sunlight. He's barefoot, she sees, and this makes her feel better. "I'm kind of a mess right now—everything's just *gone* out of my head—and they wouldn't let us on the nets for a while, so I couldn't look for you sooner ... I read about Meurig, right before they shut us out, and I didn't know if you were, or would —"

"I wasn't with him when it happened; I had just left him," he says; *it* is *my familial obligation to take care of him,* she remembers, looks up at him, concerned, but his eyes are fixed on her, his mouth is just barely smiling. Gently, slowly he puts his hands on both her shoulders as he steps closer to her. "I really had nowhere else to go, and I thought if I stayed here—but then your ship ..." He pauses, laughs a small, breathless laugh, before saying, "I've been feeling an idiot, mourning a girl I didn't even know for certain liked me at all."

She looks up at him and smiles. "I liked you," she says. The current is easing, leaving other feelings behind it. Not more manageable, but less likely to make her pass out. She thinks. "We don't really know each other, though," she says. His hands are still on her shoulders, and she can't control her own hands, now; she touches him, his hands first, then his forearms. They're strong; the skin is slightly scarred, but soft as well. She tries to focus on the words. "I mean, you probably still know me about as well as you did; it's not been that long for me, but it's been five years here—it's okay if you don't think —"

"Stay with me," he says, and his lovely accent has a frantic edge to it. "I don't want you to leave. I want to talk to you, and eat dinner, and … god, I don't know, just be near to you again—we can get to know each other, and if it's not what we wanted, we can just … stop. It doesn't have to be romantic—"

She laughs: she's standing on his stoop, half-lost in the feeling of his skin, and he's telling her it doesn't have to be romantic. He stops talking and laughs, too. "You're really here?"

"Yeah," she says. "I'd have been here before, too, if I could have."

His smile goes lopsided and fades a bit. Hesitantly, he touches her head, the short-cropped hair, tracing gently around the implant over her ear. She leans her head into his hand, feels her hair catch on his calluses.

He sounds amused, maybe a little surprised, when he says, "This is you without the mods, then?"

Now she feel nervous again. "Is it okay?"

"Are you joking?" he asks. His hand tightens just a bit as he pulls her head toward his and kisses her.

Between the current, the uncontrolled feelings, and the fact that *Ianto* is kissing her, her knees buckle. He manages to half-catch her, but loses his balance and they fall back into his foyer.

She's blushing as they disentangle themselves. "I'm sorry. I'm not usually so … swooning."

"Me, either," he says. "My ancestors would be very disappointed in my reflexes." He reaches over her to push the door closed; she catches his hand as he moves back to where he was. He smiles at her. "So. How is my accent?" he asks.

"It's really pretty," she says, smiling back because she can't not. "You're quite fluent. I'm impressed."

"Well, I had a lot of time to practice, and someone I missed very much that it reminded me of," he murmurs, ducking his head to look at her fingers, touching each knuckle with a fingertip. He glances up at her with a faint frown. "And you lost your Laendish?" he asks, concerned.

"I did," she says. She tilts her head to look at him sideways, and asks, "Could you teach it to me?"

He smiles, slow and spreading and shadowed, and says, "Yes, I can. But I'm pretty sure I owe you dinner first?"

"Dinner would be good," she says, but neither of them move into the space—the decadence—of his front room. Lia feels Ianto's fingertips on her hand and the heat of his arm sinking into her neck. He shifts, just a little, to put his face in her hair, his arms settling better around her, comfortable and fluent, like an accent or relief.

"The Lost Languages of Exiles" originally appeared in Metaphorosis
on Friday, 8 September 2017

About the author

Laura E. Price lives in southwestern Florida with her husband and son, both of whom do their best to not interrupt her as she's writing (mostly they succeed). She has degrees in English and writing from the University of Evansville and the University of Louisiana, Lafayette.

seldnei.wordpress.com

Copyright

Authors also retain copyrights to all other material in the anthology.

First appearance

All stories first appeared in *Metaphorosis*, except:

"Ligeia is Waiting" first appeared in *Perihelion*
"Cold Comforts" first appeared in *Nature*

Metaphorosis Publishing

Metaphorosis offers beautifully written science fiction and fantasy. Our imprints include:

Metaphorosis Magazine

Plant Based Press

Metaphorosis Books

Driftwyrd

Vestige

See more about some of our books on the following pages.

Metaphorosis
a magazine of speculative fiction

Metaphorosis is a weekly science fiction and fantasy magazine. Find out more at magazine.metaphorosis.com, and sign up to be notified when new stories come out every Friday.

We also publish monthly print and e-book issues, as well as yearly Best of and Complete anthologies.

Metaphorosis: Best of 2018

The best science fiction and fantasy stories from *Metaphorosis* magazine's third year.

Metaphorosis 2018

All the stories from *Metaphorosis* magazine's third year. Fifty-two great SFF stories.

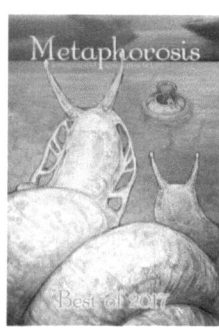

Metaphorosis: Best of 2017

The best science fiction and fantasy stories from *Metaphorosis* magazine's *second* year.

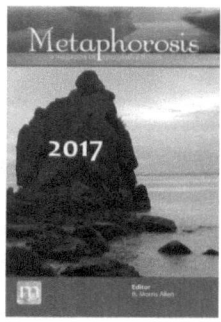

Metaphorosis 2017

All the stories from *Metaphorosis* magazine's second year. Fifty-three great SFF stories.

Metaphorosis: Best of 2016

The best science fiction and fantasy stories from *Metaphorosis* magazine's first year.

Metaphorosis 2016

Almost all the stories from *Metaphorosis* magazine's first year.

Plant Based Press

plant
based
press

Vegan-friendly science fiction and fantasy, including an annual anthology of the year's best SFF stories.

Best Vegan SFF of 2018

The best vegan science fiction and fantasy stories of 2018!

Best Vegan SFF of 2017

The best vegan science fiction and fantasy stories of 2017!

Best Vegan SFF of 2016

The best vegan science fiction and fantasy stories of 2016!

Susurrus

A darkly romantic story of magic, love, and suffering.

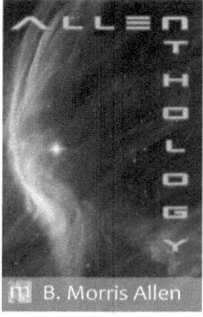

Allenthology: Volume I

A quarter century of SFF stories, including the full contents of the collections *Tocsin, Start with Stones,* and *Metaphorosis.*

Metaphorosis Books

Science fiction and fantasy books for writers – full of great stories, but with an additional focus on the craft of speculative fiction writing.

Score

an SFF symphony

What if stories were written like music? *Score* is an anthology of varied stories arranged to follow an emotional score from the heights of joy to the depths of despair – but always with a little hope shining through.

Reading 5X5

Five stories, five times

Twenty-five SFF authors, five base stories, five versions of each – see how different writers take on the same material, with stories in contemporary and high fantasy, soft and hard SF, and a mysterious 'other' category.

Reading 5X5

Writers' Edition

All the stories from the regular, readers' edition, plus two extra stories, the story seed, and authors' notes on writing. Over 100 pages of additional material specifically aimed at writers.

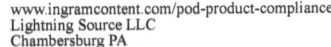